JACK BOYS VS. DOPE BOYS

Romell Tukes

Lock Down Publications and Ca$h
Presents
JACK BOYS VS. DOPE BOYS
A Novel by *Romell Tukes*

Lock Down Publications
P.O. Box 944
Stockbridge, Ga 30281
www.lockdownpublications.com

Copyright 2022 by Romell Tukes
Jack Boys Vs. Dope Boys

Lock Down Publications
Like our page on Facebook: Lock Down Publications @
www.facebook.com/lockdownpublications.ldp

Book interior design by: **Shawn Walker**
Edited by: **Jill Alicea**

Stay Connected with Us!

Text **LOCKDOWN** to 22828 to stay up-to-date with new releases, sneak peaks, contests and more…

Thank you!

Submission Guideline.

Submit the first three chapters of your completed manuscript to ldpsubmissions@gmail.com, subject line: Your book's title. The manuscript must be in a .doc file and sent as an attachment. Document should be in Times New Roman, double spaced and in size 12 font. Also, provide your synopsis and full contact information. If sending multiple submissions, they must each be in a separate email.

Have a story but no way to send it electronically? You can still submit to LDP/Ca$h Presents. Send in the first three chapters, written or typed, of your completed manuscript to:

LDP: Submissions Dept
P.O. Box 944
Stockbridge, Ga 30281

DO NOT send original manuscript. Must be a duplicate.

Provide your synopsis and a cover letter containing your full contact information.

Thanks for considering LDP and Ca$h Presents.

Acknowledgements

First and foremost, I would like to give all praises to Allah. Big shout-out and much love to all the readers rocking with me. Shout out to the West Coast Compton, 400 block, Texas, Chi-Town, Miami, and the hometown Yonkers, New York. Shout out Moreno, CB, all my Elm Street and strip niggas, my Mt. Vernon guys. The muscle gains fitness guys. Shout out to all the stand-up guys and ladies locked up in the State and Fed. Stand strong. What don't break you makes you stronger. Shout out OG Chuck from BK, Tails and Gunny, Twin Bunk Billy and Laugh. Big shout-out to the fam, Lockdown Publications, and Cash for this journey. Stay tuned, a lot more to come. You don't want to miss a second of it #Big Facts

Romell Tukes

Jack Boys vs. Dope Boys - Part 1
Who Really Runs the Streets?

Prologue

Don had Bad News, Virginia on lap with his true self he built from ground up. He and his brother K took over the City drug trade, crushing all competition.

When Don finally met his dad Rich, who was from New York serving a life sentence in Virginia prison, his life changed. Rich put Don on to his brother and ex-girlfriend, who robbed him before coming to prison.

Don and his brother K befriended Big Bio and Bree, using them as a drug connect. Once Rich found out K was fucking Bree, he told Don if he didn't kill his own brother for the double cross then there would be hell to pay. With no other choice, Don shot his own brother, leaving him for dead, unaware that he wasn't dead.

On the way to the hospital, Bree hijacked the EMT truck with K in the back and finished the job and killed K.

50 found out it was Don who killed their brother. But at the time, he didn't know K was a rat. No one did, until Don found out.

Now on Rich's good side, especially after Don killed Big Bio, their bond got stronger.

Even with serious beef in the street against different crews, Don's crew managed to hold shit down, especially when 50 came on board with his own crew.

Rich promised to put Don on to a new plug when Bree skipped town because the Feds were in town.

When Rich put Don onto a plug named Turky, who was a dirty cop trying to help Rich get out of jail by cooperating, shit went wrong.

Don ended up killing the cop and he went off to jail for a gun charge and landed in the same prison as Rich.

With Don in prison, Lil PJ and Capo held down the streets, warring with Melly, Homo, Twin, Ja, and Rock. The city prince, Don, came across Knight, who was locked up in Virginia for drug

9

trafficking. The two men eventually became cellies and built a trust-worthy friendship.

Don killed his father in the prison shower for trying to set him up. Don got sent to the hole for the murder, but an OG took the charge and Don was able to go home.

Fresh home, the news of his mother's death hurt him more than anything. The man who took responsibility for his mom being mur-dered was Rich's son from New York and a nigga name Bloody.

Don and 50 came together in the time of war to go against the Bloody crew scattered all across VA. With so many questions and thoughts, he knew he had to go all the way to New York to find out the answers he needed for his father's side of the family. While in New York, he also did his research on Bloody and killed everything he cared for.

Don met his grandfather Rick, who was a drug lord with many kids. Rich and Fats were a couple of his own children.

Rick gave Don the rundown about his rat-ass father and why he hated Rich and Don was more than glad he had killed him. Hearing how Rich snitched on his blood and stole drugs from his dad before running to the VA, he felt ashamed to be his son.

Rick started supplying Don with large amounts of coke. Mean-while in VA, Lil PJ and 50 had an FBI agent named Brock on their trail due to the murder rate and the death of the agent's family mem-bers.

CL, who was Gotti's brother, wanted the city to himself, so he tried everything in his power to get rid of Don's crew until he got whacked.

Lil PJ robbed his best friend Don and later had to pay with his blood for the double cross.

Don got pulled over with two dead bodies in his truck and was sent to the famous Riker's Island, where he awaited trial. Later, he was convicted and sentenced to 75 years to life.

When Dom found out Bree was Rick's wife, he couldn't believe how small the world was.

Bree came to visit him and pay for his lawyer because she knew Don didn't kill the people. The bodies found in Don's truck were

Rick's peoples and they were missing before Don came to New York. Bree knew Fats, his uncle, set him up, plus he was a snake type and so was she.

Bree ended up killing Rick and robbing him. Bree had plans to get some of the drugs to her cousin Lil PJ, who robbed and skipped town to start a new drug ring down south until he got murdered.

***

Knight was a known jack boy in the Bronx who robbed drug dealers and any nigga that was balling.

His crew, D Fatal, Brim, Kazzy, and Kip Loc took an oath to the streets to forever rob with no peace.

Knight's crew made a name for themselves, but when they bumped horns with another known crew of hustlers, the Bronx was never the same.

Glock sold weight under his plug, Fats, whose name was like a God in the city.

With the city in a war zone, Knight's crew started to flood the streets with work while still rapping and hustling.

Knight moved to Virginia and opened a shop down there with his uncle Slim, who was fresh home from prison after getting major time cut off his prison sentence.

Uncle Slim introduced Knight to his plug Gotti and a secret was exposed.

Gotti found out Slim got out of prison early to set Gotti up with the Feds so he could be granted freedom.

Knight couldn't believe it until he saw the paperwork and Gotti's mansion. That same night, Gotti made Knight kill his own uncle and he had no problem doing it at all.

Gotti started supplying Knight until Knight robbed his brother CL and crossed him.

Knight met a woman named Stephanie who ran drugs from D.C. to Miami. She had a little sister, but the two hated each other.

Knight sent drugs to his brother up top as they flooded the Bronx with shit.

Eventually all things came to an end and Knight got locked up for drugs.

While in prison, Gotti put a hit out on him and a few inmates tried to stab him, but Knight didn't die. A nigga named Don from Bad News saved him and they became cellies later on.

When Knight got out of prison, he went back to New York to see his loved ones dead and his little brother in the streets heavily with a vicious team.

Knight and some of his friends and family were kidnapped after Lil K got shot in the head by Money, who was Uncle Slim's son who lived in Albany, NY.

The crew was taken to Africa where they met a man Khalid, who had one of the biggest drug operations in Africa.

Khalid's son Bugatti Boy came out to explain what the purpose there was, which was to get drugs from Khalid to supply the state of New York.

The whole crew was mad at Bugatti because they felt like he crossed sides, but he had just met his dad days before them.

With Khalid as a new connect and Lil K surviving a head shot, they were able to go back to New York.

Big Blazer from Soundview was a close friend of Glock so when he got word that Knight and his goons were trying to take over the Bronx, the city went haywire again.

Money teamed up with the Big Blazer's crew against Knight, who was his cousin. Knight got an NYPD cop pregnant in the midst of a big war. Fats and Gotti both had a plan for Knight, but he became untouchable.

Lil K, Paco, Kazzy, and Red destroyed Big Blazer and his crew. Money shot Lil K's girlfriend in her head, making Red lose her memory after she killed Big Blazer.

Now the city's dope boys and jack boys were all under one roof.

Chapter 1
Scarsdale, New York

50 did tricks on his dirt bike in the back of his mansion, which sat on forty-seven acres of land.

New York was a long way from VA, but he loved everything about the Big Apple since moving up there.

The 22,271 square foot home was a four-sided brick style mansion with seven large bedrooms, five master walk-in bathroom, marble floors, elegant bubble chandeliers, walk-in closets, a family room, walk-in safe rooms, and an eight car garage full of luxury cars and dirt bikes.

50 had been in New York for six months now with his new plug, living his best life. Cindy worked back in Bad News, Virginia.

Last year, everything in his life seemed like a scary movie after losing his girlfriend Jazzy, who was the love of his life. Losing his best friend Tank Brim hit him harder than anything because they had pulled up out of the mud together. They were day ones.

With his older brother John in prison in upstate New York, 50 knew he had to hold it down and build this ship from the ground up while in New York.

50 put his dirt bike in his garage and walked inside his home to see two big booty Latina women in thongs cooking breakfast. Both of the women were strippers from the Bronx. They were sisters named Cookie and Cream. The women were medium height, sexy, thick, and eye candy.

"What's the vibes, papi?" Cookie asked as 50 walked into the kitchen.

"Y'all tell me, shorty. What y'all trying to do today?" 50 asked them, sitting on a stool and looking at their fat asses, which drove him crazy.

"Shopping," Cream told him, cooking sunny side up eggs while Cookie squeezed fresh orange juice.

"I'm down for that. But when y'all going to holler at y'all people?" 50 asked, referring to them putting him on their cousin who needed a plug in the Bronx. Since 50 was in New York, he figured why not open shop? His plug was giving him so much drugs he didn't know what to do with it.

"I'll call him today, papi, I promise," Cookie said, sitting in his lap as he slipped a finger in her tight bald pussy, which was busting out of her thong.

"Oh my god, daddy, you got me so horny!" Cookie cried out.

50 bent Cookie over on the kitchen counter, moving a bowl of fruit out of the way before pulling out his pole and ramming it into her coochie.

"Ugghhh, papi, yes," she moaned, holding on to the other side of the countertop.

"Yes, take that dick!" Cream, shouted, hoping Cookie would save her some of 50 because she loved some oral sex.

Once 50 and her both nutted, Cream turned off the stove and made her way to 50, getting on her knees to suck his pipe.

Cookie forced her sister's head up and down his side until she choked on his semen.

After that, they enjoyed breakfast and then went shopping in New York City, which was an hour away from where 50 lived in his rich upper class gated community.

***

William Bridge, Bronx

Red woke up in cold sweats, looking around a dark room and trying to remember where she was at. This had happened almost every night since she got shot in the head twice by Money in the hospital after she dressed up as a nurse to kill Big Blazer. She survived, but lost her memory after the bullet hit the portion of her brain responsible for maintaining homeostasis attached to the bottom of the hypothalamus at the base of the brain. Red didn't remember Lil K and Kazzy. She didn't even remember her own name. Lil K had been teaching Red everything over: her name, her age, her birthdate, who she was, and who her true family was.

At night she would normally have crazy nightmares and tell Lil K about them. Her dreams were of her killing people. Lil K never told her she was a cold-blooded killer just like him.

Walking into the living room in her pajamas, she saw Lil K working out shirtless in his boxers, looking sexy. She saw his manhood print and felt her private parts get wet.

"You okay?" Lil K saw her standing there, which made him stop exercising. He had been on his fitness shit lately, especially since that COVID-19 shit hit New York a while back.

"Yeah. I had another dream. This time I killed the kid," Red said with a confused look on her face.

"Are you hungry or thirsty?" Lil K walked to the kitchen, putting on his tank top.

"No. I'm just using the bathroom and going back to sleep."

Lil K made himself a smoothie and hoped the love of his life would sooner or later gain her memory back.

But he had found out Red's memory would forever be gone unless a miracle happened. He felt bad having to teach Red everything as if she was a kid. It took a little time and patience. But she had been learning quickly for the last six months. Lil K even went to therapy and to weekly mental health appointments with her so she could get better.

He still had the streets of the Bronx on lock with his brothers and his crew, even though the last year had taken the fight out of him. Beefing with Big Blazer's crew, Money, and Fats was exhausting for them all. Lil K had a feeling it wasn't anywhere near over.

The night Red got shot, Lil K was held at gunpoint by Behadi, his plug's daughter. She spared his life, which threw him off because years ago she helped save his life and heal him after he was shot in the head by the same man who shot Red in her head.

Lil K went to take a shower and then went to sleep in a different room. He didn't sleep in the same room as Red because he didn't want her to feel uncomfortable.

Romell Tukes

Chapter 2
Park Slope, BK

Bree had a million dollar condo in the classy section of Brooklyn, where she had been living for the past couple of years now. Her crib was laced out - all pink and white with fancy carpets, couches, and drapes.

Bree sat on her loveseat, painting her little cute toenails red while watching a TV show.

Last year, Bree lived a happy married life with Rick, the biggest drug dealer the city had ever seen. She left VA to get low and live a lush life with Rick, but Bree with her street mindset wasn't the housewife type at all.

When Bree came up with her master plan to kill Rick, she went full force with her plan to take over New York. Bree sent BK, a.k.a. Official, from Brooklyn out to VA to take back over the streets of VA, but her plan backfired.

Official, who went by the name BK NVA, ended up falling for a woman who turned out to be a FBI agent. Official ended up killing Brooke, a female agent, before coming back to New York. Now Official was holding down the Brooklyn streets for Bree.

After Bree robbed and killed her old husband Rick, who was Don's grandpa and Fats's father, she opened shop. Bree also found a new plug, and the product and price were unbeatable in the city.

Lately Bree had been in the gym getting her body back right because she fell off just laying around eating and getting big money.

There were only two other big-time drug dealers in the city. She had been hearing about one she hated: Fats. The other man went by the name of Knight. She also heard he did some time in the VA prison system.

Bree didn't give a fuck about any other dealer as long as they didn't step on her toes. If they did, there would be a big problem.

***
Uptown, Bronx

Paco drove up Boston Road, on his way to a car dealership to cop something nice for the springtime. Riding in trucks all summer and spring wasn't for him. He loved to show off.

Today it was a nice warm day and women were out wearing the same clothes as last year, making sure they still fit.

The drug trafficking in Washington Heights belonged to Paco and his little crew of young Dominican shooters. He ran his blocks with shooters on the roof, look-out boys, shifts, and special enforcers.

A lot had changed in six months for the young Latino boss. Paco embraced selling bricks, but he was still a jack boy at heart. If any other drug dealer had enough weight worth taking, he was still coming for it. He and Knight were vibing hard and locking down city after city now that Big Blazer and his crew were out of the picture.

Pulling into the lot full of luxury cars, Paco parked and walked up to the first salesperson he saw, which was a pretty redbone woman in a business suit.

"Good morning," the woman said, showing her white teeth and her winning smile.

"What's the vibes?" Paco shot back.

"Excuse me?" The saleswoman try not to laugh at his approach, but she had to admit he was cute.

"I'm trying to get something nice for the summertime." Paco stared at her high cheekbones and full lips.

Paco was still in a relationship with D'Aray, but another woman wouldn't hurt, plus he and D'Aray had been talking about bringing another woman onto the scene to spice it up in the bedroom.

"I may have the perfect one for you over here," she replied, taking him to the back of the lot with all the new cars.

"I think you're a perfect fit," Paco told her, making her crack a fake smile. That got serious quick.

"Your game is weak. Save it for a dumb bitch!" she spat.

"No disrespect, ma, damn."

"Don't call me ma because you will never be daddy," she told him with a serious face.

"Lighten up. It's a beautiful day - but not as beautiful as you." Paco made her crack up laughing.

"You won't give up, will you?" she said, stopping in front of a row of Audis.

"No. If I like something I want, then I won't stop until I get it."

"Okay, we'll see. But can we focus on this business?"

"Facts. I want this one." Paco said, pointing at a sky blue Audi R8 with black rims and tints.

"Are you sure you can afford this?" She checked his pockets.

"Are you ready to start this paperwork?" Paco asked, stunting on her.

Romell Tukes

Chapter 3
Uptown, Bronx

Fame Lounge had recently opened a few months back. It had been doing well for a new party spot on a strip full of clubs on Gun Hill Road. The lounge had two levels. Downstairs had a hookah area and upstairs had a bar, stage, DJ booth, dance floor, and private party sections. Knight had opened the lounge to get out of the streets for a while and he let Lil K, Kazzy, and Paco run the show.

Knight sat in his recliner in the back of his office, in deep thought about the conversation he had with Khalid, his plug, minutes ago. Khalid had raised the price on Knight starting on his next shipment, which would be there in days. Raising the price was spoken about when they first met in Africa and Khalid gave Knight his word that the price and the product would always be the same no matter what. Knight felt like Khalid tried to play him by sky-rocketing the price on him right before summer. Knight couldn't deny the fact that the coke and dope he had made the fiends go crazy all across the Bronx.

He still couldn't believe Red had lost her memory. She didn't even know who he was, which made him feel for his little brother because he knew how much Lil K loved Red.

Last year Knight went through the most beef with Big Blazer and his crew from Soundview. Innocent people were getting killed by crossfire - kids, old people, and teenagers - which made the city hot. Knight had a feeling Fats was behind everything. He found out that he had been supplying Big Blazer after Red killed Big Blazer.

Rumor had it Money had been out in Long Island and Staten Island getting big money. Knight knew that he would soon hear from him because he felt there was something boiling in a pot. The city was too quiet.

Knight hadn't heard from his baby mother since she left to get away from the mayhem, moving to the Midwest. Getting a detective pregnant wasn't his plan, but that's how shit happened. He just wished Valentine would let him be a father. But he understood Valentine's desire to guard their child and her life from his dangerous lifestyle.

Kazzy texted his phone, telling him he would be there soon.

***

Uptown, Bronx

Kazzy dashed through the Bronx streets in his sky blue Hellcat with a body kit attached to it.

Things for Kazzy had been chill since last year. He went into business with his brother with the Fame Lounge and he had plans to open a car lot near Castle Hill projects. He was going to speak to his brother about a few heavy hitters he planned to put the pressure on. He and Paco were moving so much weight throughout the Bronx, the Heights, and Harlem that they felt like Frank Matthews in his era. Lil K had his side of town on lock, but he was busy helping Red get back to herself. Kazzy hadn't seen his little brother in weeks. He made a mental note to himself to stop by his crib in Willingboro to check on him and Red because she was still the homie.

It was only 1 p.m., so when he pulled up to the lounge it was empty besides Knight's car. Walking inside, he went straight to the back as his phone started to ring. Kazzy saw who kept calling and ignored the call. He loved being single and doing him because bitches wasn't shit.

"Yo, what's the word, cuz? What's crackin'?" Kazzy shouted, throwing up his Crip set before he started Crip walking on the carpet, making Knight laugh for the first time today.

"You doing the most, son. Sit down, bro. I'm glad you here. We got some shit to talk about," Knight told his brother.

"You don't know the half! I heard this nigga Money opened shop in Brooklyn a few nights ago and he left a blood spill," Kazzy stated.

"Who run the BK besides that bitch-ass nigga Fats?"

"To be honest, I don't know, but I've been hearing about a chick and some nigga named Official, cuz," Kazzy told his brother, who had been out of the loop lately because he had been so focused on the club.

"We got another problem, bro."

"What?" Kazzy asked, hoping it wasn't no bullshit.

"Khalid raise the price on us."

"Damn, we've been keeping it a hundred with boy," Kazzy shot back, knowing Khalid could never be trusted since the first time they met.

"Facts."

"What are you trying to do?" Kazzy asked.

"I don't know yet, but I'll keep you posted. Stay on top of Money," Knight said before he switched the subject.

Romell Tukes

Chapter 4
Dannemora, NY
Clinton Max Prison

Don hung up the pay phone on the main yard, walking past other inmates on the phone. Some were yelling at their loved ones while others blew kisses through the phone to their girlfriends.

Don walked the yard with his head held high with a 75 years to life sentence on his back. It had just turned 10 a.m. so Don had to go to work in the kitchen, as he did every morning. Working in the kitchen as a cook and taking training programs kept him busy in a penitentiary. The inmates normally worked in the kitchen to survive by selling food they would steal from the kitchen. With Don, that wasn't the case. He could pay for the whole prison to go to commissary.

Don stood out in New York prison because he was from Virginia, but he got along with almost everybody. He had only gotten into three fights, this being one of the worst prisons in New York. The only thing he didn't like about New York cats was they would tell a nigga to suck their dick in a New York minute.

Bree came all the way up to the prison to see him last month. She paid for his case lawyer and his appeal lawyer, which cost her a half a million dollars in all.

Don knew he didn't have anything to do with the two bodies found in his rental car. Someone set him up and he had a few people in mind, but that wasn't his worry at the moment. He just wanted to get home.

The news of his grandfather a while back shook him, Don really liked Rick. He was an official OG. He thought Rick would kill him when he found out Don killed Rick's son Rich, who was Don's father. When Don found out his father tried to set him up with the Feds, he had no choice but to kill him.

Don knew he needed to stay focused on prison and getting back home, so he tried to stay clear-minded and not think about outside events.

As he walked into the kitchen, he saw an inmate standing around talking shit.

"Yo Lex, what's up?" Don walked up to his boy Lex from Brooklyn, whose name was heavy in the prison because of his gang status.

"I'm good, son, have a seat," Lex said, sitting at the long steel table.

"I just got off the phone with this appeal and he got a lot of hope, Lex. I just got to stay focused." Don thought about his freedom every day.

"Keep the faith, son. I got 200 years to do and eight years in the Feds, bro. I've been fighting these crackers for a decade now," Lex told him.

"Facts, bro."

"Besides that, my baby mom got me stressed out. How I call this bitch and a nigga pick up the phone?" Lex was saddened.

"That's regular shit, bro. Niggas be in jail and really believe a bitch ain't had sex in months. The day you go is the date a hoe." Don told him facts.

"I can live with that as long as a bitch setting it out, but the nigga who picked up the phone was my brother," Lex admitted.

"What?" Don knew niggas were grimy, but your own brother fucking your child's mother was the lowest.

"This nigga talking about stop calling him before he tell on some more bodies and my baby mother pregnant with his seed. Then I heard her ratchet ass in the background talking about karma," Lex stressed, trying to still soak it all in.

"You gotta stay strong. Never let people see you sweat, bro."

"I know the vibes, bro, but I'm slid to the back. I'm tapping with you later, bro," Lex said, standing up to leave.

Harara, Zimbabwe
Africa

Khalid sat up straight in his Islamic law library, staring at his daughter, who had just entered his private cave, as he called it.

"You disappointed me, Behadi. I sent you on an easy mission." Khalid's African voice was strong and powerful every time he spoke.

"I'll get him next time, Father. I wasn't well prepared for the mission, as I told you from the start," Behadi stated with her sweet voice. Behadi's face and body were fully covered in the Islamic attire she wore most of the time.

"I don't want the same thing to happen to my beloved daughter that happened to my beloved niece," Khalid stated firmly, giving his daughter eye contact.

"What do I do now?" she asked.

"Wait until my say so. Now leave," he told his daughter, who got up and left.

Khalid was frustrated that Behadi didn't kill Lil K as he told her to. Behadi's skills were some of the best. He felt as if she fucked up on purpose, but he planned to give her another chance.

Romell Tukes

Chapter 5
Long Island, NY

Kazzy leaned on his car in a Long Island diner parking lot, waiting on his homie Frank Loc. Kazzy had reached out to one of his Crips in Long Island who had some info on a nigga named Troy, who worked for a nigga named Money.

Tonight was a chilly dark night. Kazzy rocked a Fendi windbreaker to match his Fendi 'fit.

A blue Tahoe truck pulled up with rims and five percent tints.

"What's crackin', cuz?" Frank Loc jumped out of the truck - literally jumping because he was only 4'10" in height. Frank Loc sold work in the Hampstead area with this crew of Crips under their big loc Kazzy, who supplied Frank Loc with product.

"What's moving? What's the word out here?" Kazzy asked, seeing the frustrated look on his face.

"We been at war with a nigga named Troy and his crew. They all Blood under some Brooklyn nigga named Money. Word is Troy and Money out there trying to take over blocks in BK. We been going back and forth with his crew." Frank Loc had a good amount of shooters, but Troy's crew was coming hard.

"I'ma look into these, niggas, bro. I'm about to slide to Staten Island and holler at M Loc. He going through the same shit." Kazzy knew what Money was trying to do - basically slide into his hoods that didn't have a strong hold on the streets. One thing he knew for a fact was that Money knew better than to bring that shit to the Bronx.

"A'ight, cuz, get at me. I'ma hold this shit down," Frank Loc stated, turning around to leave.

"Before you go, cuz..." Kazzy stopped Frank Loc, pulling out a gun.

Boc! Boc! Boc! Boc!

Slugs tore through Frank Loc's face, knocking him to the pavement.

Kazzy got in his car, pulling off, hoping nobody in the diner saw him kill his homie.

Kazzy heard from other Crips in L.I. that Frank Loc let Troy take over his blocks, and Kazzy knew if a nigga couldn't hold down his block, then he ain't deserve to hustle.

**

East New York, BK

Money and Troy rode through Brooklyn in a candy red Lexus LC 500 coupe with tints as if they owned the city.

"You think this is going to work, bro? You know how these grimy Brooklyn niggas be," Troy stated with his seat all the way back as Money drove to a pow wow - a meeting with a group of Blood gang members he was in tune with.

"The same way we did L.I. and Staten Island, we are going to do BK," Money told his best friend.

Money and Troy had been friends for over twenty years. They were so close they called each other brothers.

Troy came home from doing twelve years a few months ago and now he was trying to lock down cities. Being from Albany and a heavy hitter from his hood, he also felt like he had something to prove. Troy hated niggas from the city because a Crip nigga from Brooklyn cut his face while in MDC Brooklyn Federal holdover.

Troy was tall, light, with Snoop Dogg dreads from the 1990s, and he had a long nasty scar on the left side of his cheek. He and Money repped the same set and both men had some ranks in their gang.

"You think all the damus going to be willing to go against Official and his people, since they got the city on lock?" Troy asked. He had heard a lot of stories about Official while in the feds.

"We about to see what's shaking right now, boy." Money parked behind a line of cars at a big park filled with Blood gang members.

The meeting lasted two hours in a public park. Money and Troy brought up every issue from the homies still locked up behind a wall. They talked about Official and a nigga named Bones. Most of the soldiers caught work from Official, but when Money cut the price on his work, everybody was on the bandwagon.

The meeting worked out successfully. Everybody was now ready to ride against whoever for Money and Troy.

Romell Tukes

Chapter 6
Manhattan, New York

Less and his girlfriend Sherri sat at Dave & Buster's eating and drinking. They went on dates at least twice a week and tried to spend a lot of time together when Less wasn't in the streets. Sherri had been standing by her man's side for years, even during his whole bid upstate in prison. The two were close friends outside of their relationship.

At the age of twenty-five, Sherri's life was in order. She had graduated college with her Master's and she worked a 9 to 5 in a dentist's office.

Less loved Sherri's dirty thongs. She was a bad bitch: dark chocolate, petite, with a heart-shaped ass, red hair, and a million-dollar smile.

"How was work?" Less asked, eating his dessert: a banana split ice cream with whipped cream.

"Busy as fuck, babe. Facts. I'll be exhausted before my break." Sherri loved her job, but at times she hated it.

"I feel you. But we are still heading to L.A. soon?" Less asked, referring to the little trip they had planned.

"I got to take off that weekend. But what did your parole officer say?" she asked.

"It's cool. I'ma holla at her this week, but we're going to be good," he told her. Less had his P.O. in his pocket, so he had nothing to worry about. His P.O didn't even give him a curfew or piss test him as other parole offices did to their parolees daily.

"Okay, good. But how about we slide back home so I can show you how much I love you," Sherri flirted.

"Shit, you can show me in the car!" Less shot back, placing money on the table before leaving.

Since being home, Less gave up his old ways of jacking, but was getting money with his crew. Selling drugs was second nature to him and he loved the hustle. Less locked down the whole Uptown section of the Bronx, including the famous Highbridge projects. His crew had the city on lock and they had been through hell and back over the years.

Losing his little brother Kip Loc to the streets and D Fatal Frame to the prison system, he knew only two things would come out of the lifestyle.

Regardless, life was good at the moment so he was just rolling with the punches.

East New York, BK

Official listened to one of his workers talking about another nigga who worked for Official and ran Cypress projects.

"I'm telling you, Official, something ain't right with son. I saw that nigga hop out Deez's car myself when I was creeping to my side bitch crib at 3 in the morning yesterday," Benny stated on the corner, posted up.

Official couldn't believe his ears. Crash was Official's most trusted worker and his own cousin. Hearing about Crash hopping out of Deez's car made him wary. One thing Official hated more than a snake was a rat. He ain't care if a nigga was blood or a close friend. He lived by the code.

"You bring Crash to me, and be able to stand on that shit you just said with your life," Official told him, walking off to his car parked across the street.

Normally Official let Bones handle all the streets while he conducted the business side of things.

Official just recently got back into real estate, buying homes and fixing them up to sell for a higher price.

Since working for Bree, his life was different. When he went out to VA under the name BK to open shop, shit went left.   Official started beefing with Don's crew, 50, Lil PJ, and Capo while dating a woman whom he found out was a federal agent. Eventually shit went left and Official had to kill the federal agent and skip town, heading back to New York.

Brooklyn was his home, born and raised. Life was rough for Official, whose real name was Kirk, but he managed to emerge from poverty and elevate to higher standards.

Official had been hearing a lot of talk about some new niggas named Money and Troy trying to open shop in his city. One thing Official didn't play was a nigga stepping on his toes, especially niggas he never heard of.

Bones texted him his location in Brownsville, so he made his way across town before he shot out to Delaware, where he had a few workers locking shit down out there.

Official was connected all over the East Coast. He never stayed in one spot too long. That's how he was able to stay out of prison. His OG told him years ago to always move around in the dope game.

Romell Tukes

Chapter 7

Richmond, VA

Gotti sat in his new soul food restaurant with his client and a good friend that was from New York. The two men had a close relationship for years. Fats made a trip to VA once a month.

"I got to tell you, Fats, you're the first person I ever met in all my years that can move so many keys a month," Gotti stated, sitting at the table, enjoying his dinner with Fats.

"If I had your hands, I'd cut mines off, champ!" Fats shot back, quick on his feet. But he knew Gotti was right.

"What's the verdict with our situation up there?" Gotti asked as his facial expression changed.

"Knight is skating on thin ice. I should have him in my web any day. He's just a hard man to keep up with." Fats had been trying to get at Knight for months, but he had no type of success, so he focused on a bag.

"Be careful. He's a smart one." Gotti couldn't help but think about the time Knight killed his goons with his crew of jack boys and robbed him in his own home.

"I know, Gotti. That bitch nigga been digging his own grave."

"Facts."

" I got a new crew opening shop all around the city trying to lock it down and my master plan is to run them niggas out of the Bronx," said Fat, drinking liquor

"I heard you got a mean crew out there?" Gotti asked.

"I got a nephew from out here up top ready to lock it down," Fats bragged, never being the type to name-drop.

"I know if I was to ask who, you wouldn't tell me anyway, so I'm going to leave it at that."

"You know how I do. But anyway, I'ma get back to New York. I should receive the shipment tomorrow?"

"Yeah, but I'm throwing a party tonight in a club I co-own with some Jamaicans," Gotti stated.

"Nah, fam, I gotta holler at my people tonight." Fats stood up to leave the restaurant, where two of his goons awaited him.

"Your loss. We going to have some bad bitches in the house," Gotti said.

"I bet."

"Facts. But I heard you made a trip to Miami a few months back to holla at Stephen."

Fats had a surprised look. "Huh?" Fats said, playing dumb.

"It's cool, Fats, but me and Stephen got a history," Gotti stated.

"History?" Fats asked.

"She is my sister. We both live different lives. Instead of being a real sister, she became an op. Enjoy your flight," Gotti told him before you left the restaurant.

Fats couldn't believe Stephen, who was one of the biggest drug supplies in the south, was his plug's sister.

***

Brooklyn, NY

District Attorney Miller walked out of his office and down the hallway, on his way to the elevator. Miller normally got off of work at 6 p.m., but tonight he had a lot of paperwork for his new case.

His name had been starting to ring bells throughout the court system for winning some big cases. One of the cases a few months prior was Don, who blew trial for two bodies in his trunk. Miller knew there was no way he had killed those two people. It didn't add up. But Miller knew he had to get a conviction because it was a big case in the media.

Walking into the lot, he saw a man exit a black BMW.

"You Miller?" the man said.

"Yes, who are you?" Miller's voice was a little shaky.

Money pulled out a gun and fired four rounds in the man's face before he got back inside of his car, pulling off.

Money had been waiting for Miller since 6 that evening. Fats asked him to do him a big solid and whack Miller for him. When

Fats gave Money the address to Miller's place of business, there was nothing else to talk about.

***

Lower East Side, New York

"Oh shit, daddy, eat the pussy!" Wendy screamed with her legs wide open as Official drained the juices out of her pussy. He sucked her clit while fingering her tightness, making her squirm and shout.

Official worked his tongue in and out of her sex box until she came again, then she returned the favor and sucked him off, swallowing his whole rod with ease.

Wendy was a Dominican bombshell with a fat ass and fake breasts to match her fake ass. The couple were just sex partners and kept each other company when she got lonely.

They made love all through the condo Official owned.

Romell Tukes

Chapter 8
Gun Hill, Bronx

Paco rode in the backseat of an Uber for the third time in his life, on his way to a car dealership with a bag full of cash.

Last night Paco wrecked his new Audi crashing into a street light in Harlem after coming from an after-hours party. The accident left him with a small cut under his left eye, so he rocked a small bandage under his eye.

Holding it down at Harlem and his hood the Heights was draining him. Being a plug was harder than he thought.

Paco paid the Uber driver and saw the same beautiful woman who showed him the Audi last time he was there. When they made eye contact, she smiled. She couldn't deny the vibes. Paco was handsome and he looked like he had his shit together.

"Well, well," the saleswoman said, looking him up and down.

"Hey, I need a new car. I crashed my shit last night." Paco looked around, seeing people shop for cars.

"Did you really crash that nice-ass car, or did you pull up just to see me again?" she asked, crossing her arms, raising her eyebrows.

"Maybe both," he flirted, finally seeing the name tag she didn't have on one last time, which read Jadaya.

"What type of car are you looking for? I see Audis are not for you," she joked.

"I want a Tesla coupe, the one with the suicide doors" Paco liked the Tesla, so he figured it was time he saw what the hype was about.

"I got you. And let me guess: that bag is full of blood money." She laughed, but she was serious at the same time.

"Why can't a young Latino man be legit?"

"Save it for a dumb bitch. I got you on the paperwork so the Feds won't be alerted, Nelly," Jadaya called him because he had a bandage under his eyes like Nelly used to wear.

"You got a lot of jokes."

"There's a lot to me," Jadaya said.

"I want to know," Paco shot back.

"You can't handle me."

"You never know until you give me a shot," Paco told her with his serious killer face.

"After we do this paperwork I go on lunch so we can chop it up," she told him, setting up a lunch date.

***

Staten Island, NY

Fats, Money, 50, and Troy all stood in a circle in a laundromat parking lot, talking about everything for the last hour.

"My hoes got a few people in the BX that's trying to get to a bag, so I'm going to meet up with them soon just so we can have a section out there, you feel me?" 50 said, seeing the three men look at each other as if it was a bad idea.

"We going to wait on that Bronx move and focus on Brooklyn, L.I., and out here," Fats said as Troy agreed.

"I heard it's only one crew in the BX. We can take that shit over too. Facts," 50 boasted, not knowing the full history between Fats's and Knight's crews.

"Give it time, bro. We going to take over. Just fall back" Money told him.

"Money, did you handle that DA nigga the right way so we can get Don home?" Fats asked.

"Yeah, and I'll take care of that other shit when that shit dies down." Money had plans to get Don home. He didn't even know Don, but Fats said he was family, so Money went to the limit for family.

"Say less. Yo, 50, sit tight. Continue doing what you doing, sending this shit to VA and falling back, until it's your time to shine." Fats knew 50 wanted to jump headfirst into the Bronx tariffs, but this wasn't Bad News, VA. He wouldn't last a day - or so he thought.

"What's popping with this Bree bitch and that Official nigga? Them niggas making shit hard in BK," Troy stated.

"Have patience with her. Trust me, she'll fall into the trap," Fats said, knowing Bree's type.

"Them Long Island Crips starting to cross, so Kazzy's our last worry," Troy said.

Their little meeting and ended and everybody went on about their life, trying to take out the streets day by day.

***

Manhattan, NY

Lil K and Red waited for one of the doctors to come back with Red's new brain scans.

"You good, sexy?" Lil K asked Red, who played in her manicured nails.

"Yes." She always kept her words short.

The doctor walked back in the room wearing a somber look.

"Go wait for me in the lobby, ma. I'll be there in a second" Lil K told Red, who looked at the doctor and Lil K before getting up to leave.

When she walked out, the doctor got right to it.

"It shows no type of improvement. She may be like this forever if the meds and surgeries don't work," the doctor said, seeing Lil K's sad face.

"Okay." Lil K stood up.

"Come back next month," the doctor said before Lil K walked out.

Lil K didn't see Red in the lobby, so he panicked and ran out front to see her sitting on the ground looking at people walking back and forth. Little K helped her up and prayed for better days.

Chapter 9
Canaan Prison, PA

"Yo, son, I'm telling you, I was the first nigga in town doing busting down Rolex watches in Brooklyn, word to the mother," a young loud Brooklyn nigga shouted in the day room.

A group of inmates paid him no mind as they shot dice in a small room. The dice were made out of soap.

D. Fatal Brim didn't gamble anymore. He would just sit back and watch and listen to niggas faking front on each other. In the federal system, prisoners gambled with flat books of forever stamps and mackerel fish pouches.

"Nigga, put your money where your mouth is!" one of the Spanish niggas yelled. He had gotten arrested for selling keys to an undercover cop.

D. Fatal Brim looked at all the stamps and mackerel laying on the floor before walking to his cell. Two minutes later, D. Fatal Brim returned with a pillowcase, walked through the crowd, and stepped on the dice, stopping the game. As he loaded up the pillowcase, everybody just stared at him, not saying a word as he jacked the dice game. The same niggas he was now robbing talked about violence and gangster shit all day. Once everything was in his pillowcase, he looked at one of the Crips, who looked like he wanted to say something, but thought against it.

D Fatal Brim walked up to an old head from New Jersey and gave him the whole pillowcase full of seafood and stamps. The old man was a legend in his Hub. He was serving a life sentence for six murders. The old head was fucked up financially.

"Thank you, young'un," the man said, already knowing how D Fatal Brim got the pillowcase because he saw him pull up on the dice game.

***

Downtown BK

Bree sat in the backseat of her Bentley while her chauffeur drove her to the local nail salon to make her 2:00 appointment. She had just gotten off the phone from hearing some disturbing news. Two of her spots were robbed last night and a few of her workers got murked during the event. Bree knew that at the end of the day, Brooklyn was shady, so trying to pinpoint who hit her spot was harder than trying to find a certain stone in a house made out of stone.

Her phone rang. She was so mad she didn't even want to answer until she saw who it was.

"What?" Bree didn't want to talk, especially to Fats.

"You next, bitch," Fats stated.

"Am I supposed to be scared, fuck nigga?" Bree asked with a chuckle to hide her real anger.

"You talk a good game."

"And I can back it up," she shot back.

"I'll see you around."

Fats's words made her laugh in his ear. "Suck my dick," Bree replied, hanging up in his face.

She knew that when blood is drawn there was no coming back.

***

Westchester, New York

Judge Santana was the judge who sentenced Don at trial. Not only was he an honorable judge, but also a great father. One of his daughters, Mita Santana, was a district attorney in the city, climbing through the ranks quickly.

On Sundays, Judge Santana went to church in Manhattan with his beautiful wife, to whom he had been married for over thirty years strong. They had five children.

He lived in a gated community in the richest section of Westchester County in a 4.5 million dollar castle. He and his wife rode in his car down to the bottom of the gate, which slowly opened.

The sunny morning set the tone for the good Sunday.

Before making it out the gate, a white GMC SUV pulled up and two masked men hopped out with submachine guns with drums. When Judge Santana saw this, he put his car in reverse while his wife yelled and screamed for her life as if the men could hear her.

Tat! Tat! Tat! Tat!

Money and Troy unleashed a barrage of gunfire that left the judge and his wife dead.

Romell Tukes

Chapter 10
West Bronx

Money parked in front of the Highbridge projects in the back section, waiting on a dancer named Pinky who had worked in strip clubs from New York to Miami.

Meeting bitches in a club was the highlight of Money's life. That's how he met his baby mother Chanel B before she got murdered by his Ops.

Pinky came out looking like a snack, wearing barely anything as she hopped in the car, smiling, knowing Money was a big spender.

"What's up, big man?" she flirted with him.

"I see you looking like a snack. What's the vibes, ma?" he asked, looking at her thick thighs.

"You da vibes," she said as he was pulling off into traffic.

A parking lot shot rang out.

Boc! Boc! Boc! Boc! Boc!

Pinky caught two head shots and fell in his lap as Money raced out of the lot.

Kazzy and Less gunned down Money's car as it sped out of the lot. They busted the windows out.

Pinky was Less's childhood girlfriend. The two were close, so when she told him about a trick named Money, he had her set him up.

Less and Kazzy jumped back into the truck, pulling away from the projects.

"You had to kill Pinky?"

"Fuck Pinky. We just missed this nigga." Kazzy was pissed.

"Pinky had the best pussy a nigga ever had, fam, word to my mother, boy," Less stated seriously.

"Your mind still fucked, I see." Kazzy shook his head, thinking about how he let Money get away.

***

Manhattan, New York

Mita took a few days off of work for her parents' funerals. Her father, Judge Santana, held weight in New York and his death sparked a nationwide manhunt.

Weeks before her dad's death one of her co-workers, Mr. Miller, a local DA, was murdered. Mita wondered if there was any type of connection between the two murders because the style of the killing was the same.

After the funeral, she planned to start her research on the murders herself.

***

Brooklyn, New York

Official and two cars full of shooters made their way to a small project called Auburn PJs.   Official heard a new crew was trying to take over this side of town where he sold weight and he wasn't going for that. Once he got to the projects, he saw eight new niggas posted up around the building looking like they were hustling. Official got out of the car with a shotgun pump and locked eyes with Troy sitting on the bench smoking.

When Troy got a clear view of the shotgun, he got ghost.

Boom! Boom! Boom!

Troy's crew didn't last a second as Official's crew surrounded the projects, gunning them down.

Boc! Boc! Boc!

Official chased two niggas around the projects, gunning them down with ease.

When the place was clear, Official and his crew of hitters scanned the block twice before police arrived.

Chapter 11
Jersey City, New Jersey

Uncle Pimp's glass mansion had a wide range of women: black, white, Latina, and Asian. Uncle Pimp's name in the pimp game was like Jay-Z's in the rap game and Michael Jordan's in the NBA.

At forty years old, Uncle Pimp looked younger than most men in their 30s because he took good care of himself. Thanks to his lifestyle of daily sex and lush way of living, he was able to do as he pleased and live a stress-free life.

His home had over twenty women in it who were loyal to him, willing to do whatever for their pimp and the man they called God.

The mansion had twelve bedrooms, each room shared by two women. One room was Uncle Pimp's headquarters, and the other room was a guest room.

Uncle Pimp had saved most of the women from sex trafficking. They were homeless women, lost and confused women, and women who fell in love with him. He took good care of the women, getting their bodies done, clothing them, educating the ones who had no education, and being more of a father figure than a sex partner - or as most would call it, a pimp.

Growing up in the Brooklyn streets, he used his looks to get what he wanted out of women at an early age. As he grew up, his mind leveled up and built the mind frame of a true pimp and drug lord. By the age of sixteen, he was pimping hoes from the East Coast to the West Coast. Never once did Uncle Pimp make a woman sell herself. Instead, he brainwashed them into thinking sex freed the hurt, pain, and rage they carried within.

When he stepped out of his room in a white Armani suit, there were six women guarding the double doors with assault rifles. To his left, he saw his Haitian goddess named Cassey and to his right was a beautiful Syrian woman named India. Cassey and India were his most trusted and dangerous soldiers. All his women were taught how to fight in hand-to-hand combat and to use weapons.

Today Uncle Pimp had a meeting about drugs with one of his clients. Normally he would send one of his women to handle his business, but this time he wanted to make a special appearance.

"Good morning," Uncle Pimp said to all of the women before walking downstairs to eat his breakfast.

***

Bronx, New York

50 had only been to the Bronx a few times and he loved the vibe, so the South Bronx it felt like home.

Cookie and Cream drove him through the mean streets of the Bronx, taking him to their cousin's crib because he needed a plug. The Bentley pulled up to the curb, parking in front of a small house next to a Benz coupe that belonged to Frenchy Kid.

"When we go inside, let us talk please. His English is bad, but he gets to that bag," Cookie stated, exiting the car with her sister and 50 following her.

Frenchy Kid opened the door with an assault rifle in his hand and a crazy look on his face, not letting them inside. He looked 50 up and down, wondering what the fuck his two shady-ass cousins had going on bringing a black nigga to his crib.

Cookie and Frenchy Kid talked in Spanish for a minute. Their voices went from high to low as she tried to explain that 50 was the plug he needed to expand his network.

Frenchy Kid was young with a serious crew and had a section of the Bronx on lock. The only problem was that he needed a plug. His last plug got killed in a carjacking in Soundview.

"How can you help me?" Frenchy Kid asked, looking him up and down.

"You mean how can we help each other?"

"Whatever, papi," Frenchy Kid shot back in his terrible English.

"Let's talk in the back," 50 said in Spanish, shaking both women and Frenchy Kid because he was just popping shit about 50 in Spanish.

50 took Spanish class in school so he knew how to speak it somewhat.

***

Harlem, New York

Paco and Jadaya lay in Paco's king-sized bed, sweating and drained. Their date had turned into drinking, then it led to sex.

"You're amazing," Paco told her. Jadaya's pussy was the best he had in a long time. Her shit was super wet and tight.

"You beat my little coochie up like that," she joked, but she was also dead-ass serious.

"I'm trying to go for round two."

"Oh hell no you ain't. Not tonight." She got serious before letting him go down south on her bald, plump pussy.

Romell Tukes

Chapter 12
Brooklyn, New York

Judge Johnson was one of the few black judges in the Supreme Court in Brooklyn. He recently received Don's case weeks ago and it was up to him to overturn it or uphold it.

Judge Johnson lived in Middletown, New York, basically an hour and a half away from where he worked at. Normally he parked in the court parking lot, but today it was jam-packed with cars so he parked down the block at a daily parking lot.

Walking down a dark street with his briefcase, he had no clue a commercial van was parked across the street watching his every move.

A man in a hoodie approached Judge Johnson, exiting a nice luxury car.

"Excuse me, but do you have a light on you? I'm waiting on my wife and I forgot it in her purse," the innocent man added.

"Sorry, young brother, I don't smoke," the judge stated, seeing a man with a brown blunt hanging from his lips, knowing that had to be weed.

"Say less."

"Are you smoking weed in front of a courthouse?" Judge Johnson asked.

"Yeah, why? Do you want to hit?" The man acted as if the blunt was already lit.

"No. I'm going to call the police." Judge Johnson pulled out his cell phone, but before he could dial a number a metal pipe smashed into the back of his head, knocking him out cold.

The white commercial van that'd been parked across the street pulled up. Three men tossed Judge Johnson's body into the back before racing off.

Money climbed into his luxury car, burning rubber, tailing the van to their secret location in Bed Stuy.

***

Bed Stuy, BK

The van and Money pulled into an empty factory with no widows near a river.

"Get his ass out," Money told his soldiers hopping out of his car.

His crew opened the side doors. Judge Johnson was hogtied with duct tape around his mouth. Judge Johnson was awake and moving, but he didn't see anything because a pillowcase covered his face.

Money took the pillowcase off his head and the duct tape from around his mouth.

"What's going on? I'm a judge. I have a family. You have the wrong person."

"I know who you are, Johnson - or should I refer to you as Judge Johnson, a.k.a. Uncle Sam." Money hated any type of law enforcement, especially judges. If it was up to him, he would have been killed Judge Johnson, but this mission was a favor for Fats.

"I don't understand what this is truly about. I've done nothing wrong." He looked at Money's goons, but they paid him no mind.

"That appeal. You got David Wilson serving a 75 to life sentence in the state," Money stated, seeing the judge's face, knowing it was a fresh topic.

"I know about it. But what does that have to do with this?" Judge Johnson's stomach was flat on the floor, making it uncomfortable to breathe.

"I'ma need you to do whatever is in your power to get him released."

"What!" the judge shouted.

"You deaf?" Money shot it back.

"I can't do that. I can lose my job."

"You can also lose your family also. You pick. Untie him," Money told his goons before pulling away from the scene.

Judge Johnson was so scared he didn't even call the police. He was a Brooklyn nigga to the core. He knew what he had to do to keep his family alive, and calling the police wasn't it.

Chapter 13
White Plains, NY

Kazzy drove through Westchester County. Today he wanted to find a nice condo in the upscale area, which wasn't too far from the Bronx. Since Knight had been in Miami for the past couple of days, Kazzy Loc had been the one taking care of business affairs. A new shipment had arrived last night and he split it amongst Paco, Less, and a few of the most trusted workers. Kazzy's mind had mainly been focused on Money and his crew. He wanted to spill their blood, but making so much money distracted him from his priorities.

As he pulled up to a brick building in a classy neighborhood. He called the real estate agent he met online as he walked into the building. He took the elevator to the thirteenth floor.

The hallways were wide and spotless. As he walked down the hall, he saw the real estate agent, who was a tall skinny white woman, talking to one of the baddest bitches he had ever seen.

"Mr. Wilson, I'm sorry about this, but one of my clients showed up a little early. Is it okay if I show the condo to the both of you?" The woman looked at them both.

"I don't mind," the beautiful woman stated, looking at Kazzy, sizing him up.

"I'm down," Kazzy said, peeping at the cutie checking him out.

"I'm Cassey," the women introduced herself while the white woman walked off to start the tour.

"I'm Kazzy."

"This is a nice spot," Cassey stated, walking behind the real estate agent.

"Hell yeah." Kazzy looked down at the white marble floors.

"These are cathedral ceilings. Here we have a three-sided fireplace, cherry cabinets…" the real estate agent said, walking into the living room area.

"What's the rent going for?" Cassey asked the question the woman had been hiding on both phone calls.

"3,700 a month, but it's well worth it. We have a stone terrace Jacuzzi inside the master bedroom and a private gym in the lower section of the building."

Kazzy and Cassey both looked at each other and turned to leave at the same time, laughing on the way out.

"That bitch high," Kazzy said in the elevator.

"Nah, I smell liquor on her breath, so I know she is drunk," Cassey said, laughing.

She and Kazzy made eye contact. He loved the sparkle in her hazel eyes.

"I got something on my face?" she joked.

"Naw, you're just sexy and I want to take you out to dinner," he shot his shot at her.

"Right now?" She sounded shocked, but she couldn't deny the vibes.

"If you let me?" Kazzy got off the elevator, walking with her into the lobby.

"Where are we going to go?"

"Let me handle that," Kazzy replied.

"Okay, whose car we taking?" she asked, looking at her BMW coupe.

"Mines," Kazzy told her, opening his car passenger door for her.

"Cute. A true gentleman." Cassey was blushing.

The dinner date went amazing. Kazzy took her to a romantic spot in the city. They spent hours getting to know each other and laughing.

***

Clinton Prison, NY
Four weeks later

At 6:40 a.m., most inmates were sleeping in a cell, exercising, or just getting up.

Don laid on his bunk watching TV, waiting to start his day. He had a daily routine: wake up, breakfast in the kitchen, come back to the block, get ready for outside rec in the yard, exercise, then go to work in the kitchen after showering in the bath house in the yard. After work, he would go to the library to study his case and new case laws that could help him.

"Move on!" a prisoner yelled from his cell located in the front of the tier.

When inmates yelled move on, it meant police were coming down their tier so everybody could stop sharpening their knives, put their drugs up, or stop jerking off.

Don saw four correctional officers coming his way on his fun-house mirror hanging out the bars of his cell.

"You. Pack your shit. You're being released," the prison warden said with an attitude, chewing on tobacco and spitting the juices on the floor.

"Me?" Don had to make sure he was hearing the warden clearly.

The warden looked at his paper and told him to hurry the fuck up.

Don couldn't believe it. He must have won his appeal. He packed up all his important shit and gave all his commissary to his neighbor.

Romell Tukes

Chapter 14
Queens, NY

Troy brought his little sister, Logan, down from Albany to spend weekends with him. She was a cute dark-skinned slim woman with low esteem due to the cross-eyes she had, but no one could deny her beauty.

Yesterday while doing a little shopping on Jamaica Avenue in Queens, she met a cute dude and bagged him. That day they had plans to chill at a hotel smoking and drinking then, maybe hit up a club. But Logan had different plans now because she just got off her period and needed some dick.

Walking through the hotel, she looked at herself in the mirrors, admiring the way her dress fit her curves. She forgot the nigga's name she came to see, so she looked at the recent text message where he had texted the room number and told her the door was unlocked.

Logan took the elevator to the seventh floor and made her way to the room through the long narrow hallways. Logan opened a door to see Larry with his shirt off opening a bottle of Henny.

"Hey," she said, walking into the hotel room, staring at his chiseled abs.

"You look cute. Come here," Larry said as she followed.

Logan then did what she knew best and got on her knees to give him the best blow job he ever had. Anytime she sucked a nigga's dick, they would stalk her. She wrapped her thick phat lips around the tip of his manhood after pulling out his snake.

"Ummmm," she moaned, making her way up and down on his rod.

Larry's eyes rolled around in his head, loving her porn star skills. Larry knew she was ugly, but he also knew ugly bitches had the best pussies and oral sex.

"I'm about to cum."

"Cum in my mouth, daddy," Logan said, sucking faster and faster until she felt his body vibrate.

"Let's hop in the Jacuzzi." Larry lifted her up from the ground.

"Wait until you hit this coochie," she bragged knowing what she had between her skinny legs.

The Jacuzzi in the bathroom was filled already with bubbles and water. Logan stripped down, showing her flat chest and hairy pussy, but Larry liked her little curves.

"I want you to fuck me raw from the back first," she demanded.

Larry got inside the large warm Jacuzzi and bent her over. As he slowly entered her, the firm grip of her pussy walls prevented him from going deep into her. "Relax," he told her.

"I'm tight," she moaned, unable to take the dick.

Larry gripped the back of her neck and drowned her. Logan tried to restrain herself, but Larry was too strong. Two and a half minutes after drowning Logan her body was lifeless, and she floated on top of the water.

Larry got out of the Jacuzzi and got dried off with the hotel towel. Larry's real name wasn't Larry. He had only used that name to bag Logan.

The killer's name was Less. He saw Logan with Troy a couple of times and he assumed she had to be his wifey, so he kept a close eye on her and made his move.

Less, Paco, and Kazzy were on Money's ass and now Lil K and Red had recently come back in the field. Shit had been a little better.

***

South Beach, Miami

Knight had been in Miami for a few days now while his crew held shit down in New York. His reason for being in Miami was simply that he needed a new plug. He couldn't go to Stephen because he heard she skipped town due to federal indictments within her own circle.

Knight knew a childhood friend who now lived in Miami and was getting a bag, so he promised Knight to put him on to his connect. Knight had been waiting for an hour now for the plug to show up, but nothing had happened yet.

"Fuck this shit," Knight mumbled to himself, taking his drink and leaving the outside bar area, heading to his rental car.

As he walked back to his car, he saw a sexy Latina woman leaning on his car and playing with her nails. It was a little dark out, but Knight knew his eyes worked.

"I like the way you move, Knight. My people speak highly of you," the woman said in her soft voice.

"Who am I speaking to?" Knight couldn't lie; she was a bad bitch.

"That's not important right now. How about we go talk? My goons are parked down the block. They're going to follow us to my mansion. I'm driving. Pass me the keys," she shot back.

"What's your name, ma?" Knight asked, passing her the keys.

"Julie. You want to know my Social and age?" she shot back.

"Maybe."

Knight and Julie were talking and vibing all night and making business arrangements.

Romell Tukes

Chapter 15
Newark, New Jersey

Knight drove down the famous Prince Street, which used to be the worst area in the city back in the days. Since coming back from Miami, he had a full-blown A-1 plan, and the only way it was going to work was if he took his time because it could backfire. Now with Julie on his team tucked in the cut, he knew he could put his plans in motion.

He pulled onto a dark block full of row houses, most of them torn down, run down, or abandoned. It wasn't hard for him to find the house he was looking for because it stuck out like a sore thumb with a Lexus coupe parked in the driveway.

Before Khalid's son Bugatti Boy got murdered, he and Knight had a long talk and Bugatti Boy told him everything he would ever need to know about his father from doing his own research. Knight took everything Bugatti Boy told him and stored it in his brain for a rainy day, and a storm was soon approaching. Bugatti Boy told Knight that Khalid had a few family members in the States and advised him to stay on popping.

Uncle Pimp was Khalid's brother. Only few knew this, but now that Knight did, he was a target. Knight had a lot of people in New Jersey, so he did his own homework on the man they called Uncle Pimp.

Only a few people knew Uncle Pimp had a few children and an ex-wife. One of his children played college basketball, but normally stayed in Newark with his mom instead of living at the college dorm in Philly.

***

Dammi cooked dinner for herself and her lazy son Rob. Dammi turned over the fried chicken while turning down the heat on the stove so she didn't burn shit again. This was her everyday life: work, home, and sleep with no type of social life whatsoever.

Dammi stood 5'3", brown sugar complexion, thick in all the right places, and a cute youthful face that drove men crazy. At forty, she was still a bad bitch, but her life wasn't all peaches and cream. She grew up in Newark and met Uncle Pimp, thinking he was her shining armor, but he turned out to be a vicious pimp after they married. She became his main whore and sold her body for his own financial pleasures. When she got pregnant years later, she gave up the life of sex trafficking to raise the son she had with Uncle Pimp and got a divorce.

Hearing the doorbell snapped her out of her daydreams.

"Rob, get your lazy ass off that game and get the fucking door. You're nineteen and still playing video games!" she shouted, hoping her son would change his ways because he was a mama's boy and spoiled.

When she didn't hear anything, she walked out of the kitchen, thinking it was one of Rob's gangbanger friends. She didn't want them in her house and around him.

"Rob, who——" Her words paused when she saw her son lying on the floor with a gun pointed at his head.

She looked at the handsome man with the long dreads and shiny grill, seeing he meant business.

"I just want to know about your ex-husband?" Knight asked calmly.

"This is how you ask people shit?" she shot back, really looking at her crying son.

"Yeah," Knight repeated, looking at her and how beautiful the woman looked.

"Pimp is a mastermind. He brainwashes women into doing what he wants He's rich, nasty, shady, and he lives in Jersey with his gangs of whores. That's all I know. I hate him with my soul. He fucked up our lives." She got louder, shedding a tear.

"Thanks." Knight didn't want to end it in blood, but he had to.

Knight shot Dammi twice in the face then her crying son in the back of the head twice also.

***

Jack Boys Vs. Dope Boys

Lower East Side, NY

Don loved the feeling of being a free man again. He had a new outlook on life. He wore suits and he planned to open a small business and a phone store. Today he planned to open a business bank account and try to get a loan because he still had A-1 credit.

He was spending a lot of time with 50 and Fats, making big plans to take over the New York streets. 50 was still flooding VA with dope, so now it was time to expand.   50 still had concerns about who put him in prison, but he planned to put that in the back of his head for now.

Don was on his phone standing in the line in the bank when a woman bumped him, knocking his phone out of his hands.

"Oh, I'm sorry," the woman said, picking up the iPhone that just came out.

"It's okay." Don saw how beautiful her appearance was and got stuck.

"Nice phone," she told him, handing him his phone back.

"It would be nicer if it had your number in it," Don flirted.

"I see you got a little game." The Latin woman blushed.

"You call it game, but I call it honest," Don replied. She rocked a business suit also.

"I like that. But take my number and call me any time after 7 p.m. I don't normally do this, but I did knock your phone out your hand," she said, giving him her phone number.

"Maybe you should knock it out my hand again," he shot back.

"Don't push it, cutie pie."

"Hold on. Before you go, what's your name?" Don asked, seeing her turn to leave.

"Mita," she said before walking out of the bank to get back to the DA's office.

Don was really starting to like New York now even more. The mixture of women was like Miami and he loved it.

Romell Tukes

Chapter 16
Manhattan, NY

Fats had been having a secret love affair with Barbara for ten years now. The reason why their love life had to be discreet was because her husband was the NYPD Chief of Police. For a white woman, Barbara's body would give a black woman a run for her money. Not only was it real and soft, but she wasn't sloppy.

Twice a week she would skip work to meet up with Fats at a fancy hotel in Manhattan near the Hudson River. Her husband had no clue about it. She would arrive an hour before her lover to set up the room the way he liked it. She always made sure the room had fresh candles, fruit, condoms, and a romantic ambiance. Every trip they would use room 409 because it was one of the four suites and had the best views in the morning. There was nothing like getting fucked from the back with the sun beaming on her face to her.

Inside the hotel, she took the glass elevator to the fourth floor, excited for today. The only thing she loved more than black cock was her two grown children who lived in Boston, where she grew up.

When she got to the suite, she used the room key card to swipe herself in as she did every time. The room drapes were all closed, giving the room a dark vibe. She closed the door and turned on the lights, walking inside. When she made it to the living room, she saw a beautiful woman dressed in all black sitting on a couch. Barbara knew this day would one day come, so she took a deep breath, trying to hold in her fear.

"You're his wife?" Barbara asked.

"Bitch, please sit down." Red pulled out a gun from under her thigh.

"Oh Lord." Now Barbara was shaken to death.

"Don't panic." Red was kind of puzzled as she tried to remember what Lil K told her to say at this point.

Red had begged Lil K to put her back in the field because she was having dreams about killing and robbing people. She told him if he would let her do things she used to do, her memory may come back. At first Lil K was against it until her doctor basically told him the same thing.

"I have money in the bank and my jewelry is all real," the woman stated.

"Tell me about Fats - and don't give me erroneous bullshit," Red said, sitting back to listen like she was in a therapy session.

Barbara spent forty minutes telling Red everything she knew about that. She hoped he would show up early, but that didn't happen.

Red used a silencer on her Glock, shooting Barbara eight times in her chest before walking out smiling.

This had to be the first time in a long time Red really smiled. She felt fantastic and on cloud nine.

***

Brooklyn, NY

Kazzy rode in the truck with two of his Bronx niggas on his way to East New York.

"Fade, you sure these are the niggas? You can't trust these Brooklyn cats," Knight said from the back seat, texting Cassy, the woman he had met a few weeks ago.

"Yeah, son. Luck G a solid dude, bro. When he told me he works for the Money nigga, I explained to him we had some beef with son and needed his help," Fade shot back while driving to the projects, where Luck G was waiting on them.

"Okay." Kazzy trusted Fade because he had known him since they were little niggas running around the Michelle projects and Millbrook.

When they pulled up to the block, the projects were empty. Knight felt something was totally off.

"It's 1 p.m. and this shit is a ghost town," Kazzy stated.

"This is his building right here," Fade said, parking before getting out the driver's side and making a call, leaving Kazzy and X9 in the car.

Kazzy saw Fade whispering on the phone while peeking at Kazzy. Being a street nigga, Kazzy checked his surroundings to see six shooters come out of a store across the street with guns.

"X9, slide in the driver seat," Kazzy told his homie in the passenger seat before jumping out with a Draco.

Kazzy aimed his weapon at Fade first, hitting him four times for the double cross, then he shot it out with the shooters. Kazzy didn't let go of the trigger as he hit three shooters, taking them off their feet. The shooters all had handguns. Nobody was ready for the Draco's magic.

When Kazzy saw Troy run off, he got in his truck and X9 pulled off, looking at Fade's dead body, disappointed.

Romell Tukes

Chapter 17
Washington Heights, NY

"Daddy, do you have to go? I'll do that thing you like? D'Aray lay back under the warm covers, naked, watching him get dressed.

"Ma, don't do that. I've been cooped up in here with you all day," Paco shot back, placing twin Desert Eagle pistols in his waistband.

"We don't get to spend time with each other no more. It's always me, you, and Jadaya." Her voice gave out a hint of jealousy.

"I thought she was cool and fun when she was eating your coochie," Paco joked.

"It's not about sex, Paco, you know that." She got serious.

"When I get back, I'll do whatever you want," Paco told her, giving her a kiss. Paco loved how sexy she looked without makeup, unlike other women who looked like monsters without shit piled on their face.

"Okay. I believe you."

***

Lil K saw Paco come out of his building dressed in all black with a skull cap and gloves.

"What's shakin', my guy?" Paco got in the car.

"About time." Lil K pulled off.

"How's Red doing, bro?" Paco asked, knowing that was a soft emotional topic for him.

"Cooling, ready to kill shit. Basically she's starting to remember shit now, at least," Lil K replied, getting on the highway.

"Good. Take your time, bro. Trust me, she'll get well," Paco said thinking about the mission at hand.

***

Harlem, NY

Money had taken 50 and Don out for a night on the town with a few goons to show them a good time. The hookah bar was closing, so everybody was leaving.

"It was turned up," Don said, following the crowd outside.

"Facts. I told you." Money followed a group of big booty girls outside.

50 was drunk, but still cautious. He had left Cookie and Cream home because he wanted to spend time with Don.

Outside, Don saw the crazy look on Money's face when two niggas ran across the street with guns.

Don and 50 had both left their guns in the car, but Money was strapped.

Paco and Lil K sprayed rounds at Money's crew, almost hitting 50, but shooting two of Money goons instead.

Money busted back while everybody yelled and screamed, running from bullets. When Money grazed Lil K, he thought he had them.

Suddenly, police lights could be seen coming down the street. The shooting stopped and everyone went opposite ways.

***

East New York, BK

"What's goodie, son?" Bones embraced Official with a crew of six-shooters behind him, coming out of the Pink House building.

"I heard our boys got into a big shootout in Harlem last night." Official smirked, blowing weed smoke into the wind. Lately Official had been so busy trying to hold down his city from other dealers trying to steal his turf that he ain't got no sleep. The heavy bags under his eyes spoke volumes. While Bree was in Miami on vacation, he controlled everything for her.

"With who?" Bones asked.

"I don't know, but I'm going to find out because it seems we are not the only crew in the city who wants Money's blood," Official said. He had spent hours trying to figure out who else had it out for Money.

"I'ma ask around, homie. We are about to slide to Queens to handle some shit, son. Get at me later," Bones told Official, who got a text from his wife telling him to pull up so he could eat her ass.

Romell Tukes

Chapter 18
Southside Queens, NY

Bones came out to Queens to drop off some money and drugs to his homie Auto, who just came home from doing a long bid up top. Pulling into one of the most dangerous projects in Queens, he made sure his gun was fully loaded. It was dark out tonight, so Bones knew to keep his eyes open. He knew how Queens niggas got down, especially after they got at his favorite rapper Chink Drug.

Business in Brooklyn was booming. The money was coming in so fast that he didn't know what to do with it. Last night he tossed $70,000 at a strip club in Brooklyn with his goons, showing out and shutting shit down.

Bones texted Auto, telling him to come outside, as he parked in the back in the parking lot 4. There were so many skyrise buildings he felt like he was stuck in a maze.

When he saw Auto and a man in a black hoodie walking towards him, he grabbed the book bag out of his backseat to see his longtime friend.

"Yo, big bro, what's up?" Auto asked.

"This for you." Bone handed Auto the backpack full of money and drugs. When Bones and Auto's friend locked eyes, shit got different real quick.

Auto's friend was Troy, and when he recognized Bones, there was no turning back. Both men reached for their weapons.

Bloc! Bloc! Bloc! Bloc!

Bones's gun went off first, but Troy slipped behind Auto, who didn't have a clue what was going on.

Auto's body was shaking with bullets as Troy and Bones went at it in the darkest section of the parking lot.

Boom! Boom!

Troy missed Bones's head by a few inches.

Bloc! Bloc! Bloc!

Bones fired toward the van Troy was ducking behind.

Suddenly, Bones's Desert Eagle jammed. Troy took advantage as he jumped up, firing hollow rounds at Bones.

"Fuck B," said Bones, climbing into his car and peeling off, running over Auto's dead body.

Troy got out of the parking lot, running to where he had parked his car.

Troy and Auto were like brothers. They did time together in Green State Prison as youths. Troy had kept in touch with him ever since.

Auto told him he was about to introduce him to his boy, but Troy had no clue it was going to be Bones.

***

North Miami, FL

Bree hated coming to Miami. It used to be fun growing up living in VA then going to Miami to turn up, but that shit got played out quick. Now she loved taking trips to Paris, overseas, and to private islands. Miami was for basic bitches, in her books.

Today Bree had to meet up with her plug, so she waited in a restaurant bar in her expensive Seasons 1 hotel. Her connect would always meet her in public areas, which was smart, but Bree preferred private settings.

She has been dealing with her plug since killing her husband Rick. Her people had the best coke and dope she had come across in a long time with a good price range.

While Official held the streets, she was trying to figure out a master plan to take care of Fats, who was trying to step on her toes by sending Money and Troy into Brooklyn. Bree heard their names all over the city, especially in the area where a lot of Blood gang members were at, which was all over. She heard Don was out of prison. She hoped he wouldn't let Fats brainwash him as he did everybody else.

As she took a sip of water, her connect walked in, looking like a true model in her all-white attire. Bree looked at Julie and couldn't help but be jealous of how beautiful the Latina woman was. If having any sexual relationship with a female ever came to Bree's mind, there was no question that Julie would be number one on her bucket list.

Bree and Julie laughed, ate, talked business, drank, and went to have a girls' day out at a nice spot to get good peace of mind.

While that was taking place, Julie's men were driving tons of coke up to New York in an 18-wheeler for Bree.

Chapter 19
Uptown Bronx, NY
Weeks later

50 walked down the stairs of the apartment after talking to Frenchy Kid about his next shipment and the details of how to pick it up from an abandoned factory in Brooklyn in a few hours. Frenchy Kid had been moving close to sixty keys in two to three days in the Bronx alone, which was unheard of to him. 50 had been hearing the BX was a gold mine. He thought it was all talk and cap until now.

Don went to VA for a few days to tie up some loose ends, he told 50, who had no clue what that meant.

Cookie and Cream had a few people in Yonkers, Mount Vernon, and Newburgh they wanted to see about making some big money. 50 had to use his GPS system to get him around when Cookie and Cream weren't around. The city was so big that 50 got lost almost every day.

This morning, the weather was humid from the rain shower last night.

As he walked out of the building, the first person he locked eyes with crossing the street was the man he saw at the club last week. 50 never forgot a face, especially after they shot at him, almost taking his life.

***

Paco got a call from one of his workers saying some nigga named Frenchy Kid was moving heavy weight on his block, so he came to see Frenchy Kid. As he got closer to the building, he saw a familiar face, but couldn't quite make it out. When Paco saw a gun appear in the man's hand, it hit him who he was: the li'l nigga from the club who was with Money. Paco dipped on the side of the building as 50 sprayed at him.

Boc! Boc! Boc! Boc! Boc!

"Goddamn!" Paco shouted, seeing a little boy get hit in the crossfire.

People started to scream and cry, but they weren't going anywhere near the little boy bleeding to death.

Paco aimed his gun around the brick wall, firing wild shots, but 50 had already disappeared. With not much time, Paco ran past the crowd of civilians crowding around the little boy, who didn't make it. Once in his car, he peeled off down the block, promising to kill that little nigga. Paco could tell the shooter wasn't from New York because of the way he held his gun and his baggy clothes. Paco had to go pick up Jadaya and D'Aray from the hair salon downtown, so he put what just happened in the back of his head.

Jadaya and D'Aray had been spending a lot of time with each other since realizing they'd have to share Paco. Things were starting to perk up in an intimate way between the three of them. Paco was starting to feel like a pimp again. But every day he thought about Kathy and Haley, his ex-lovers who got killed. To this day, he never met gangsters as loyal as those two. He would place new flowers on their grave at least once a week.

***

The Village, NY

Kazzy took Cassey to a nice lounge, bar, and restaurant establishment for a night out on the town on a first date. They were doing a lot of texting and talking, but tonight was the night of the truth.

Cassey looked alluring in her red designer dress, showing a lot of skin and her crazy curves. She caught the attention of every man in the room. Kazzy rocked a Dior two piece 'fit with some jewelry. His attention wasn't so much on Cassey but on the brother on the upper lever in the booth with a cute Spanish woman getting up to leave.

"You okay? You haven't touched your food at all," Cassey said since, something was very wrong with Kazzy. Red flags went up in her head.

"I'm sorry, Cassey, this is bad timing, but I need you to take my car keys drive yourself home. Leave now. I'll call you later." Kazzy handed her his Porsche keys and she got her purse and left.

Once Cassey was gone, Kazzy got up from the table, leaving 400 hundred dollars on the table. He rushed outside and saw his target with the Spanish woman, laughing. Kazzy crept towards Money and his girl with his weapon out. Money saw his new side piece look back and yell, making him turn around to see Kazzy with his gun aimed.

Bloc! Bloc! Bloc! Bloc!

Money's girl caught stray bullets to her temple and two in her cheeks. Trying to save himself, Money got low, rolling under cars to avoid being shot, getting dirt all over himself. Money had his weapon in his trunk, but Kazzy was coming so hard he knew his chances of getting to his AR-15 assault rifle were slim.

Bloc! Bloc! Bloc! Bloc!

The gun barked in the parking lot, setting car alarms off. Kazzy didn't see Money until he saw the red Benz racing out the other end of the lot. Police sirens could be heard, so Kazzy ran off, hoping to see a cab, but instead he saw Cassey.

Kazzy got inside as she drove off like a speed demon.

"Thanks."

"I want another date," she said before turning up the true name song on the radio "I Can" with Kelan.

Romell Tukes

Chapter 20
Park Slope, BK

Don had his face buried between Mita's legs, sucking on her swollen clit. Mita had one of the prettiest pussies he had ever seen in his life. When Mita came over to his condo for a dinner date, things got sexual real quick.

"Ohhhhh my fucking God almighty, I'm about to cum! Yesss, suck dat pussy!" Mita yelled as if she was trying out for *American Idol*.

Don had his finger in her split with his mouth focused on her clit, making it hard for her to control her climax.

"Mmmmmmmmm!" she gasped for air as she came hard. Cream poured down her coochie and inner thighs.

"You ready for this dick again?" Dan whispered before seeing red dots of blood staining his sheets.

As soon as Mita saw it, she jumped up like a bat out of hell. "I'm so embarrassed about my period coming on! I have to go." Mita got dressed.

"It's straight, shorty. Why you trippin'? This regular shit," Don told her, taking the sheets off his king-sized bed. Don had fucked her missionary and from the back minutes ago and busted two nuts on her. Mita was the real deal. Don admired her body and class. Mita was wifey material.

"I'ma leave. I have to wake up early for work," she said, grabbing her purse. Mita had told Don she worked in the courts and he took that as if she did filing work, unaware she was one of the top D.A.s in New York.

When Mita left, Don called 50 so they could prepare to meet up with Fats for the big shipment he had waiting for them.

Money explained to them that they were into it with some Bronx niggas. When Don heard this, he wanted to reach out to his boy that he did a bid with from the BX named Knight. Don decided to wait until the time was right to reach out tonight. When they were cellies in VA, Knight told him so many stories about the Bronx. He wanted to ask Fats if he had heard of Knight, but decided against it. He knew niggas be lying in jail all day but when they get out, they really be nobody and broke.

The condo Don lived in was very expensive, but it was worth it. There was a pool, gym, and a spa downstairs for all the residents. The lower garage had its own level with 24/7 security guards to look over the billion-dollar building.

Don left his condo on his way to Westchester County to get 50 and his two bitches he now traveled with. Don needed to talk to him about that because he didn't trust a woman whatsoever.

***

Alabama Projects, BK

Official had the Bamas on lock. It was one of the grimiest projects in East New York, but Official loved it. Last night Official had his crew divide up the bricks he got from Bree, who was on her way home from Miami.

"What the vibes, homie?" K-Bands asked Official, who crossed the street, walking to his car.

Official had just come from checking on his trap as he did twice a day to make sure shit went well. "Yo K-Bands, what's this shit I'm hearing about you ratting on Smalls and them niggas?" Official asked K-Bands, whom he grew up with and had known since he was a little nigga out on the corner selling nicks and dime bags of dirt weed.

"Who, me?" K-Bands looked scared.

"Yeah, you, bitch-ass nigga!" Official upped his gun. "Snitches get dealt with." He fired two shots, hitting K-Bands in the center of the forehead with both.

Official walked off, leaving a worthless snitch nigga dead.

Chapter 22
New Jersey

Uncle Pimp woke up early every morning before his women to exercise and meditate to start his days off with positive energy and vibes. Today was a little different because he had to go pick up some of his dead daughters' family members so they could attend the funeral that would be held tomorrow. Being a vet in the game he was able to connect the murders of his son, ex-wife, and his daughter together.

He sent two of his most trusted women in the streets to find out who was responsible and he came up empty-handed. India was looking for answers in New Jersey and he sent Cassey to New York. Both women were expected back any minute. Just as the thought came to his mind, they walked through the front door. Uncle Pimp turned on his large flat screen TV in the living room as India and Cassey walked inside, looking like models.

"Hey daddy." India rushed to give him a hug.

"What you got for me, baby?" Uncle Pimp said, looking at both women.

"I couldn't get nothing, daddy. Nobody knows shit," Cassey stated.

"How about you?" He looked at India, trying not to get frustrated because he wanted the killers who murdered his family.

"I got nothing in Jersey, but I slid out to the Bronx and a man named Knight been inquiring about you to some major people," India said.

"Knight, huh?" Uncle Pimp sat down, trying to let it all soak in.

"I tried to look for him, but the only thing I know is he had a girl," India said.

"I want the both of you to stay in New York at the condo and do whatever needs to be done to find him. Am I making myself clear?" Uncle Pimp kept his attention mainly on Cassey.

"Yes, daddy," both women stated before leaving the mansion.

***

Williamsburg, BX

Lil K spent the night on the couch. He never shared the bed with Red because he knew she wasn't in the right state of mind. Since she was killing, things around the crib had gotten a little better for them communication wise.

Being a light sleeper, he felt someone standing over him. He woke up to see Red standing there ass naked.

"What's wrong?" he said in his sleepy voice, sitting up with an erection in his boxers.

Without any words, she climbed into his lap, lowering herself on his dick. Her sex muscles gripped the tip of his rod as she worked her hips.

"Ugghhhh," Red moaned while kissing his lips, letting him grab her hips and fuck the living hell out of her.

Lil K felt her juices all over his lower body. Red came hard, creaming his manhood with her juices before she spun around, his dick still inside of her. Lil K let her bounce her ass on his pole, feeling her tight grip.

"Yes, right there!" she cried as he hit her G-spot back-to-back, making her nut seconds before him.

After the couch fuck, they went to the bedroom, where it went down like old times.

***

Bed-Stuy, BK

Troy had a little crew selling work on Myrtle Avenue down the street from summer projects. Six hustlers were posted on the strip, cutting each other's throats when it came to the fiends.

Boxy ran a block and they had work for days. The only issue was the niggas up the street hating from Thompkins projects. They'd been back and forth nonstop shooting for two weeks now. A body was dropping every night.

"Let's get a dice game going, fam," Boxy said to his little cousin, sitting on a few milk crates, listening to music on a small Beats speaker.

"Who got the dice, son?" Nino said, looking around, seeing three unfamiliar faces walking up the block.

"Who dat?" Boxy asked, looking up the street.

Bloc! Bloc! Bloc! Bloc!

Boxy got hit up first, then his whole crew all tried to dash in different directions.

Nino caught two bullets to the head, dying in front of the store, bleeding from his head.

Bones and his goons ran up the block, heading back to East New York, smoking loud and drinking early in the morning - a Brooklyn thing.

Romell Tukes

Chapter 23
South BX, NY

Don waited for his good friend to arrive in the hotel parking lot on River Avenue across the street from the police station leading into the Highbridge section.

Last night Don called the number Knight had given him while they were cellies in prison in VA. The number belonged to Knight's brother Kazzy. The two men had a long conversation, each unaware of who the other truly was. Kazzy gave Don his brother's number so he could call him. When Don called, Knight was so happy that words couldn't describe it, but when Don told him he was in New York, he couldn't believe it. They agreed to meet at the hotel and made plans to help a club that just opened up nearby.

A black Tesla two-door coupe pulled up, but when they saw the diamond grille shining in the car, he knew who the man was. Both of them got out of their cars, embracing each other.

"Damn, bro, I see you doing it just like you said," Don stated, checking out Knight's chain and diamond bust down AP watch.

"Yeah, no capping, son. I told you a nigga really checking a bag. I miss your crazy ass, boy. I'm glad you beat that jail body," Knight said, shaking his head, remembering when Don stabbed up his own dad in the jail shower.

"Real shit, man. OG Ice took that charge for me. That was love. I send him and his family money every month." Don said, knowing that he would've been serving a life sentence had Ice not taken responsibility for the jailhouse murder.

"That's what's up. But what brings you to my hood?" Knight had to ask.

"I've been up here for a while, bro. I got some family up here and shit. I just came home from up north. I gave the system back 75 to life on my first appeal."

"Oh shit, bro, that's wild!" Knight couldn't believe it.

"I got set up in Brooklyn with two bodies in my rental," Don told him, still trying to look past someone setting him up.

"I'm glad you're out. But you still on a bag or what?"

"Hell yeah! I got a mean plug in BK. We got a little crew locking shit down," Don said proudly.

Knight had only heard of a few plugs in Brooklyn. He wondered who Don was copping from, but he didn't want to be nosy.

"That's litty," Knight shot back.

"Yeah, and dude family, so I'll get them things at a good price."

"Them Brooklyn niggas be grimy. Just be careful."

"Facts. We got some beef with some niggas out here. I wanted to ask you, but I don't know too much detail about them, only the little bit Fats told me."

Don's words caught Knight full of attention.   "Fats?"

"Yeah, you heard of him? He my uncle. He's good business." Don saw Knight's face and body tighten up. Don saw Knight whole vibe change up in seconds and he knew something was very wrong.

"You on the wrong side," said Knight as everything started to add up in his head.

"What you mean?"

"I'm that Bronx nigga out to kill Fats and Money," Knight told him.

Don didn't even know how to reply. He looked across the street to see police everywhere, so shooting Knight would be a death sentence.

"So I guess it is what it is, bro." Don looked Knight in his eyes.

"I guess so. I'll see you around," Knight said, turning his back on him and walking to his car.

Neither Knight nor Don could believe what just happened. A good friendship just went down the drain. They knew in war there were no such things as friends and peers.

***

Manhattan, NY

Less and Sherri went out on a date at a new BB King restaurant located next to a few clubs they planned to hit. Since Less came home, he had been trying to lay low and stay focused, but with so much going on with his guys, he couldn't sit back and watch.

Jack Boys Vs. Dope Boys

He spoke to his crazy brother last night when on a jail call and he told Less to leave the streets alone, because the real niggas were dying or going to prison with a rack of time. Sitting here looking at how beautiful Sherri was made him want to put a seed in her and fall back from being a true jackboy, but he knew it wasn't happening.

Romell Tukes

Chapter 24
Red Hook, Brooklyn

"Word for mother, son, the only reason why the little homies ain't smoke them fools is because they were all damus, you feel me, son?" Dekil stated.

Official listened to what his boy was saying because Dekil always kept it real with him. Hearing how he let Money and a crew of Blood gang members come to Dekil's hood and ask to share the turf Official controlled didn't sit too well with him.

"You let them niggas walk out of here because they were Bloods?" Official asked.

"Official, you knew what I was when you first met me. That's not my fight. I fuck with you on the money tip, but I can't go against my people," Dekil said, looking at people come in and out the back of his building as they talked near the playground area.

"A'ight, and I understand." Official turned to walk off and then he stopped and pulled out his gun.

Boc! Boc! Boc! Boc! Boc!

Dekil didn't even see this coming as bullets opened his chest, making him stumble backwards until he hit the ground. Official shook his head, walking off with Bones awaited him.

"What happened?" Bones said when Official got in the car.

"Pull off. Dekil out the picture. Call Black Lo and tell him Red Hook is his until further notice, son." Official knew Dekil could not be trusted, so he eliminated any doubt.

"It was that nigga Money?" Bones asked, really sick of hearing about him and his crew.

"Yep." Official looked out his window into the Brooklyn streets he loved to death, refusing to let anybody snatch it from him.

***

Uptown, Bronx

Knight called a meeting with the whole crew to update them on what was going on in a local basketball court open to the public at all hours of the night.   Everybody had five minutes to show up before it hit 12 a.m.

Knight couldn't believe Don was down with Fats. This threw a big foul in the game because they used to call each other brothers. Never in a million years did Knight picture Don being Fats's nephew. Since Don was on the other side then he will have to stand his ground through the bloodshed. Last week Kazzy had burnt down one of Fat's establishments.

A line of luxury cars sped into the lot along with a motorcycle Red rode on. Knight realized Red was starting to come back to her normal self, but there were a few things still off. When Lil K told him the only thing she wanted to do was kill, he knew Red needed help that she could only get from healing and time.

Kazzy, Paco, Lil K, Less, and Red all entered the basketball court to see Knight sitting in the middle like a true boss.

"This shit feels like the old days," Kazzy said, thinking about Fatal Brim, Kip Loc, and Black's rat ass.

"Everybody good, I hope?" Lil K asked.

"The money is great, but things about to get nasty out here again," Knight said.

"What do you mean?" Less asked, not trying to go back to jail already.

"What it sound like, scared-ass nigga?" Lil K added, looking at Less.

Lil K felt like Less had been on some funny shit since he had been home, as if he was scared to get his hands dirty.

"Nigga, you got a problem with me or something, homie?" Less started approaching Lil.

Red reached for her gun, but Kazzy gave her look let her know it was okay.

"You want a problem?" Lil K shot back.

"Y'all do that goofy shit later. We got some out-of-town niggas trying to take over our city and y'all about to bite each other's heads off," Knight said.

"Money will be taken off." Kazzy stated.

"It's not Money. He got some VA niggas with Fats's nephew."
Knight saw a few shocked faces.

"Who?" Less asked

"My old celly I was locked up with named Don. He had a serious problem too, so now we have more problems," Knight added.

"They must have been with Money the night we got into the shootout," Paco said, thinking about the club shootout.

"I know they are in Brooklyn beefing with niggas named Official and Bones." Less repeated what the word on the street was.

"I want you and Lil K to get up with them niggas so they know what's up, and maybe we can work together with them BK niggas," Knight stated.

"Got you," Lil K said.

The crew talked for a while, unaware of the eyes watching them from afar.

Knight had another reason for coming to Philly, but right now, he rode in the back of the Uber on his way to the airport. The Uber driver was a cute young dark-skinned woman who didn't say much, but she found his diamond teeth interesting.

"You can drop me off right here, Miss," Knight said as she pulled into one of the airport's car lots.

"I can drop you off at the entrance. That's a long walk," she said, stopping her car.

"Nah, this perfect." Knight's words sent chills down her lower back.

Knight pulled out a 9 mm Taurus with a silencer attached to it. When she saw the gun, she wanted to scream, but her lips couldn't move. She didn't keep cameras in her Uber because she felt like there was no need to invade people's privacy.

Six hollow tips went into the back of the woman's head, killing her. Knight realized that she had no cameras in her car, so that was a big plus for him.

Knight walked to the dumpster and wiped the gun off with his shirt before tossing it in the dumpster.

The woman he just killed was Uncle Pimp's daughter. Knight wanted to send Khalid a message in an anonymous way by attacking his brother's family.

Chapter 25
186th Street, Bronx

Paco ordered the number six on the McDonald's lunch menu, texting Jadaya, who told him to come pick her up from work later or to tell D'Aray to. For the past few weeks Jadaya and D'Aray had been getting more sexual with each other than him and he wasn't having it at all.

Things were about to get heated in the city right before winter. Paco couldn't wait, but he was hearing a lot about this Frenchy Kid stepping on his turf. Paco ran a couple of his workers off his corner last week and killed two of them, which made the block hot with police.

Coming out of the fast food restaurant, Paco stared at one of the baddest bitches he ever laid eyes on. Paco opened the door for her, looking at her perfect thick frame and her pussy print. The woman had Middle Eastern features with a Latina look.

"Thank you," the woman said in a soft voice.

"Anytime, if given the chance." Paco saw her face light up with joy.

"Excuse me, but what do you mean by that?" The woman stopped in the doorway.

"I would like to spend some time with you."

"You don't even know me," she shot back.

"I'm trying to get to know you. So what's your name?" Paco asked.

"India. I have a half hour lunch break, so how about we go sit down and talk? I don't think it would hurt," she said checking out his jewelry and gear.

"Sure." Paco knew he had somewhere to go back to, but India made him forget.

The talk was supposed to last thirty minutes, but turned into an hour. They planned to get up later.

Paco called D'Aray to tell her to pick up Jadaya from work on Gunhill Road because he would be busy.

***

Manhattan, NY

Mita had been working day and night on criminal cases at work and also the slaying of her dad, Judge Santana. She got ahold of the video footage from the gate entrance of her father's mansion and watched it over sixty times. Yesterday she sent a copy of the footage to a crime lab so they could take a better look at it. Mita saw two faces, but they weren't clear on her computer.

When the phone rang, she rushed to pick it up, talking to the crime lab. They gave her two names.

The system had the men's street names and government names. Mita hung up and punched Money's and Troy's name into the system put an APB out on them both for the murder of her father.

***

Brooklyn, NY

Less had his Brooklyn nigga Will, whom he had did a bid with upstate, reach out to Official and Bones for a sit-down.

Lil K sat in the passenger seat as they drove to Crown Heights in silence. The two hadn't spoken since they had words at the meeting with Knight.

"This how it's going to be?" Less spoke.

"Nigga, what?" Lil K got on the defensive quick.

"I'm saying though, bro. I just came home and I'm not trying to go back to jail, bro. I want a better life, so I'm going to leave the game alone when all the shit is over," Less stated, pulling into the projects.

"How come you ain't been saying that? I thought you were on some other shit, bro. You made your bones in the game. I got mad respect for you, son, plus the shit is getting played out." Lil K laughed, but he knew in this life, there was no getting out.

"Good luck, boy. You know how we are rocking. But let's handle this shit," Less said, looking at the two niggas waiting in front of a project building.

Official and Bones saw Less and Lil K approaching them. Will, who worked for Official, told him some Bronx niggas wanted to reach out to him and he asked who. Hearing Less's name, he knew this was Knight's crew.

"What's good, bro? I'm Less and this Lil K," Less introduce them.

"I'm Official and this is Bones. Good to meet y'all. I've been hearing about y'all for a while in these streets," Official stated.

"Likewise, bro. Knight couldn't pull up, but we thought it would be good if we do this Bronx to Brooklyn vibe to go against Money, Fats, Don, and them."

Lil K's words confused them.

"Who the fuck is Don?" said Bones

"Fats got his nephews up here from VA," Lil K stated.

"Them bitch-ass niggas is trying to take over y'all hood too?" Official asked

"They are trying," Less said seriously.

"We can team up, fam. We can slide out there and y'all can slide out here," Official told them.

"Say less, bro." Less turned to walk off.

"Tell Knight our boss said she hopes to meet him soon. She likes to network." Official repeated.

"Who is dat?" Lil K asked.

"Her name Bree," Official told him before walking back into the projects, where millions of dollars were stashed.

Chapter 26
River Avenue, Bronx

Less pulled up to Sherri's mother's day care, where she worked when she wasn't at her job in the dentist's office.

The past couple of weeks, Less and his team had been in Brooklyn, trying to get a lead on this Don character. Things with Sherri had been a little awkward lately because Less's focus was on the streets and not her. Less felt fucked up about the vibes because he knew it was his fault. Every day while in prison he used to call home and tell her how he planned to leave the streets alone, but then after coming home, he jumped in them head first.

Tonight Less had picked up some flowers and chocolate for her and had a nice dinner date set up.

Waiting on Sherri to come out, Less saw two badass Latin women walk up the block smiling at him. Less got out so they could see his Cuban link chains choking his neck on top of his Dior outfit. Before he could get a word out, Sherri came out of the daycare and caught him looking at the two nasty hoes walking up the street.

Less quickly grabbed the flowers to see what his girl was staring at like she had seen a ghost. Seeing 50 come out at him with a handgun, he went into motion, dropping the flowers and candy and going for his gun.

50 shot Sherri in her upper chest, knocking her to the ground.

When Less saw this, he went crazy and started spraying in 50's direction. The bullets were coming so fast that 50 took off down the block, where Cookie and Cream awaited him.

Cookie and Cream had walked past Less seconds ago. They were to distract him from the real mission.

Less rushed to Sherri's aid.

"I got you, ma, just breathe. Please, daddy, got you." Less lifted her up with ease to take her to the hospital a couple of blocks away.

***

Atlantic City, NJ

Kazzy had come out to AC with Cassey, spending the weekend at the most expensive hotel on the East Coast.

They had made their relationship official a few days ago after spending a lot of time together. Kazzy hadn't been in love in a long time, but he knew Cassey would be his final.

"You ready to hit this casino, baby?" Kazzy asked Cassey, who was in the bathroom putting on makeup and getting dressed.

Minutes ago they had made passionate love all through the hotel room. Cassey even told her that he loved her. Kazzy told Cassey everything about his lifestyle and who he really was with no cuts.

"You good, baby?" Kazzy put on his shoes to see why Cassey didn't reply.

Entering the bathroom, he saw her in a beautiful black dress, pointing a gun at him and crying. Tonight was the night Uncle Pimp wanted her to kill Kazzy. She was updating Uncle Pimp on everything except one thing, and that was her getting emotionally attached.

Kazzy looked into her sexy eyes to see so much hurt and pain in her eyes. He knew by the way she aimed her weapon that this wasn't her first time about to kill someone.

"If it's worth anything, I really do love you, so let me die with honor," Kazzy told her as tears rolled down her face.

"Fuck!" she shouted. She dropped to the floor, crying like a baby.

Kazzy held her, still with the gun in her hand.

"Talk to me, Cassey. It's okay. You safe," he told her, sensing she feared something.

"He sent me to kill you and your crew for killing his family" Cassey said through tears.

"Who?"

"Uncle Pimp in Jersey," she told him, wiping her tears.

"So he sent you, and you must be one of his...." Kazzy didn't want to call her a whore, but he couldn't find a word to replace it.

"It's okay. I'm one of his hoes, but I don't sell pussy. I'm his enforcer, and so is India, who deals with your friend Paco," she said.

Kazzy knew he had to warn Paco. "What are you going to do?" Kazzy had to ask her.

"I'ma be here with you. I love you, Kazzy. I never felt this way about anybody. Uncle Pimp got me and my baby sister from Haiti and took us and basically made us sex slaves." She held her true emotions as she told her story.

Kazzy sat there with Cassey for hours listening to her story and she made him cry. Hearing Cassey's whole story made him fall in love with her more. She opened up to Kazzy, telling him everything about herself and Uncle Pimp. Cassey explained to him that Uncle Pimp would use her sister as ransom for people's deaths so she had no choice but to kill on his demand. Kazzy couldn't believe this. She explained to him how dangerous he was.

"What about your sister?"

"I don't know, Kazzy. It's your life or hers, and I told you I can't kill you," she said sadly, knowing her little sister was just as good as dead.

"We will figure it out. Let's go to bed."

He helped her up, leading her to the room, where they made real love, looking into each other's eyes.

Romell Tukes

Chapter 27
Morris Heights Med Center, BX

Less hadn't left Sherri since she had been shot last night. Seeing her laid up in the hospital bed made his blood boil to the point of no return. He knew it was his fault she got hit up. Sherri was a good woman and she didn't deserve what she got. Less always felt Sherri deserved better than him. She made the trip up north every weekend, sent food packages, money orders, letters, and pictures daily, and putting her through the jail stress made him feel less of a man. She stood tall during his struggles. He told her everything and leaving the streets alone was a start.

Looking at Sherri slowly open her eyes made him smile. The pain meds had her knocked out for the past couple of hours.

"What's up sexy?" Less asked while rubbing her long red hair.

"Did you call my job?" Sherri asked, hoping she didn't get fired because she was supposed to go to work today.

"Covered."

"Thanks, but I'm going to kill your ass when I get out of this hospital bed," Sherri said in a little voice because her upper body was still in pain.

"I know, babe. I'm sorry. I just hope you will forgive me."

"I thought you said you was leaving the streets alone?" She looked at him with a disappointed look.

"I am, Sherri. There are a few things I have to clean up first love. This isn't like a real 9 to 5 job. I can't give a two weeks' notice." Less knew she would never see things from his view because she wasn't a street chick.

"You lied to me." Sherri's eyes got glossy as she thought back to the times he used to tell her he wasn't going back to the streets.

"I'm sorry, Sherri, but I couldn't leave my brothers for dead," Less admitted.

"So they are more important to you than me? They drove eight hours every Saturday to see you? Did they have sleepless nights like me? I'm pretty sure they ain't wait until you came home to have sex. Maybe I'm just the dumb bitch," Sherri stated, in tears.

"I can't see my life without you, Sherri, and that's why I want to tie the knot. Sherri Jacque, will you marry me?"

When Sherri heard the words "marry me", she thought she was being pranked or something. "What?"

"Will you marry me? I'ma go get you the biggest ring and spend the rest of my life with you," Less told her.

"Yes, I will marry you - after you leave the streets alone," she said seriously.

"Deal." Less kissed her crusty lips. "Your breath stinks," Less joked with her.

"Boy, shut up and get me the fuck out of here." She was ready to go. Her injuries were minor, more or less flesh wounds.

***

Uptown, BX

Kazzy and Paco both pulled into the Fame Lounge parking lot at the same time to meet Knight. Kazzy was glad to see Paco so he could fill him in on what Cassey told him.

"Yo, what's the vibes, dawg?" Paco said, hopping out of the foreign car.

"We need to talk." Kazzy walked into the lounge to see workers cleaning up preparing for a big party tonight.

Both men walked to the back, where Knight waited for them.

"What's up with the gang?" Knight said, in good spirits today.

"We need to talk. That's why I called this private meeting" Kazzy stated.

"Where are Lil K, Red, and Less?" asked Knight, wondering why the whole crew wasn't present if Kazzy had called a meeting.

"They are busy. But let me get to the point. I met this badass Haitian bitch a while back and we hooked up. I took ma to A.C. just to get out of town. We were in a hotel room and shorty got a gun pointed at me crying" Kazzy said.

"I remember those days," Paco said, shaking his head, having experienced that many times.

"Bro, you called us here for that?" Knight had better things to do than to listen to Kazzy love stories.

"Listen. She didn't want to kill me, and I knew she was a real killer by the look in her eyes. She told me Uncle Pimp sent her to kill me and to get to you." Kazzy sat there looking at Knight.

"He on to us," Knight stated.

"Who's Uncle Pimp?" Paco asked.

"Let me finish, son, damn. As me and an old girl vibing, she told me her life story and how Uncle Pimp uses her sister as a ransom so she'll do what he tells her to do. He also sent another bitch at us," Kazzy explained.

"Only a dummy would get caught slippin' like that, no offense." Paco laughed, wondering how Kazzy could be so slow and naive.

"Well, I guess you dummy of the year because the bitch he sent is fucking with you: India, some Middle Eastern bitch." Kazzy saw the look on Paco's face and he knew he hit a vein.

"That bitch! Her pussy was too good to be true." Paco had fucked India twice and couldn't get enough, but he knew she had a secret life. He thought she had a man or something.

"Y'all need to handle the females and we're gonna pay Uncle Pimp a visit, but I got a plan in the making with this Khalid clown. I'm just waiting on the perfect timing. Uncle Pimp is Khalid's brother and they got the game fucked up," Knight said.

"Thanks for telling us now." Paco got up and walked out.

Paco was really mad at India for letting her play him. Normally he would smell shit like this a mile away.

Romell Tukes

Chapter 28
Fulton Avenue, Bronx

Lil K drove through the city like he owned it, on his way to visit his dead homies' gravesites. Blue Banger and KP Loc's graves were located in the same cemetery, so he wanted to kill two birds with one stone. He asked Red if she wanted to come to Banger's gravesite, but she told him no because her memory of Banger was blurry. Lil K thought maybe if she came that old memories would come back to her, but all she wanted to do was kill and have sex now. The sex was crazy, but at times he felt like he was taking advantage of Red because of her condition.

While passing Claremont Park, he saw a familiar face that made him pull over and grab his H&K handgun with a 30-shot clip.

50 had come out to drop off some work to Frenchy Kid's workers in a parking lot next to a church and the police station. Cream waited in the car while 50 talked with the man named P Dud.

"Tell Frenchy Kid on the next load we will square even, family," 50 Cent said as P Dud closed the trunk of his BMW full of keys.

"I got you, son, say less," P Dud said, turning to walk off until he heard someone yell something.

"Look out, 50!" Cream yelled out the car window before the shots started to pop off.

Boc! Boc! Boc!

50 ran to his left as Lil K's bullets hit P Dud all in his neck.

"Don't run!" Lil K yelled, letting shots off at 50's people. His gun was inside his car.

Cream saw that her man needed help and tossed 50's gun to him out the car window. When Lil K saw Cream, he fired four rounds at her, hitting her in the head, killing her.

50 saw Cream go out and picked up the weapon which had landed in front of his feet.

Boom! Boom! Boom!

50 hit Lil K in his left hand before seeing police running out. Lil K saw the police run into the lot and took off on foot. When he

reached his car, he hopped on and sped off, making a clean getaway. Minutes later, he got on the highway, bleeding lightly from his hand. He saw he had only gotten grazed so that wasn't too bad, but it still hurt.

***

Brooklyn Heights, BK

Official's wifey called him to pick her up from her mom's house in the middle class area of Brooklyn.

Official had to meet Less in an hour so they could go put in some work in the Flatbush area.

Last night Official got word that some Blood cats were selling keys for Money over there, and Official wanted to spin the block and catch them slipping. He had to make it known he ran Brooklyn and outsiders weren't allowed.

Bree had asked him to get up with her tomorrow and he told her he would, plus he was running low on work.

Last week he had copped a mansion upstate towards the Newburg area for him and his girl, but she still wanted to come to their BK crib.

Driving down the block, he saw his wifey standing there talking to somebody. He could tell she was trying to tell them "No, I'm good" by her body language. As he got closer, he saw who the man was and parked in the middle of the street.

When he got out and locked eyes with Money, it was too late. He blew Official's girlfriend's brains out all over the sidewalk.

Bloc! Bloc!

Official sprayed the block up while Money moved quickly in between cars to get back his own shot. Money saw he had Official in a tight spot in the middle of the sidewalk and shot him twice in the thigh before running off down the block.

Money knew the woman belonged to Official so he had asked her where he was, and she refused to tell him. When he saw Official, he killed her first as Official came out at the right time.

Official limped to the car and followed Money, but he couldn't keep up with Money's car because of the blood loss.

Bones's auntie lived around the corner so Official double parked in front of her crib and limped inside.

The bullets had gone in and out so he was okay, but just lost a lot of blood.

Bones's auntie saw him at her front door. She took him in and stopped the blood and cleaned his wound up good.

Romell Tukes

Chapter 29
Downtown Brooklyn, NY

Bree waited for Official near a nice riverfront. It was a whole strip full of restaurants and bars open to the public. She had been meaning to catch up with Official, but she had been a little busy trying to open a hair salon in Manhattan.

A new order of coke was supposed to arrive tomorrow so she wanted to make sure he was prepared.

Bree knew Don was in her city with Fats trying to take over. She hoped it would not ever have to come to this, but she put her business first. She hadn't seen him yet, but she knew if she did it wouldn't be nice. After coming so far in the game, Bree refused to let it be snatched away by some suckers.

An all-black Lamborghini pulled up and Official got out with his blue Yankee cap low.

"Hey you," Bree said, giving him a light hug, smelling his strong Gucci cologne.

"How are you?" Official asked, seeing her wearing a tight Dior jumpsuit.

"Thanks for coming because I've been super busy trying to open the hair salon downtown," she explained.

"I already know."

"What's going on in these streets?" she asked seriously, because the last time they talked, it was about Fats and Money. Now with Don and 50 in the picture, they needed more help.

"They've been hitting our spots and trying to take over our spots, but you know how I'm giving it up."

"You know, gonna hold it down." She nodded, knowing how Official got busy.

"They were also trying to make their way into the Bronx so the BX niggas reached out to me," Official said.

"Knight?" she said with excitement, because she had been hearing his name for years.

"I met up with his people and we formed a crew. Dem fools solid and with that shit." He knew working with them would be like taking candy from a baby.

"Great." She smiled.

"I told them you couldn't wait to meet Knight." Official saw Bones calling, but he didn't pick up.

"Keep me posted on what's going on," she told him, checking her lady's Rolex watch.

"Okay, but what's up with the work? I'm running low." Official only had forty-seven keys left.

"Oh yeah, tomorrow be ready. We got a big load," Bree said, walking off towards one of the bars to get a drink.

***

Money saw a bad-ass bitch walking off. It was dark so he couldn't make out her face, but when he saw Official walking back to his car, he knew it was now or never.

Minutes ago, Money had come out of one of the bars after having a few drinks and saw Official getting out of a new Lambo. Money rushed out of his truck, which was parked across the street from Official.

Bloc! Bloc! Bloc!

The bullets missed Official as he got to his weapon from his lower back to shoot back six rounds.

Looking at Money, he got mad and emptied out his whole clip, making him run back across the street. When Official ran out of bullets, he jumped and his Lambo raced off, glad Bree didn't get caught in the crossfire.

***

Miami, FL

Knight took a private jet to Miami to pay Julie a visit to talk about the first shipment. Knight's plan was now in full motion. He was going to rob Khalid and be ready to face whatever came with it. Robbing Khalid was his plan all along, but he wanted to find a steady plug first before jacking Khalid. Knight did his full research on Khalid before he chose to pull his move.

Julie came into his life at the right time. He would have to separate business from pleasure because she was a bad bitch.

When his jet landed, his limo service was waiting for him. He planned to stay at a five-star hotel for the weekend. Knight was starting to feel bad for leaving his brothers and homies for dead in the streets during a time of war.

Knight knew he had to focus on the business aspect of things like the lounge and drugs, because if he didn't, they would have to go back to nothing and go backwards. That wasn't an option. Seeing Don on the opposite side of the field hurt him because he had built a strong bond with him in prison.

Knight saw the limo driver open the door for him to get inside the limousine. It wasn't the service he normally dealt with, but he played it cool, knowing something was wrong. Once inside, he saw a woman in a miniskirt, looking beautiful. When he got a full look at her, he didn't know what to say.

"Knight, you look good," Stephen said with a glass of Moet in her hand.

"Stephen, where you been at? You look fine as fuck." He couldn't help but speak his mind.

"Thanks."

"How did you know I was coming out here today?" Knight asked as the limo pulled off.

"I have my ways. I'm disappointed in you," she said.

"Why?"

"Now you're dealing with Julie?" She sounded upset.

"Stephen, I had nowhere else to turn. I just cut off Khalid."

"You could've waited for me," she said.

"Waited?" He laughed.

"Yeah."

"I had no clue where you went. You just disappeared," he said, seeing she wasn't trying to hear that shit.

"I had to lay low. Shit got hot. I'm good now."

"I see," Knight said, looking at her sexually but trying to control himself.

"Hold on. You cut off Khalid?" she asked to make sure she had heard him right.

"Facts."

"Knight, it don't work like that. Khalid will hunt you down and kill you. He has a lot of ties to powerful people." She wondered how stupid he could be.

"I don't care about that. I robbed him, and that's it. He can get it back in blood," Knight said seriously.

"You have no clue what you just did, Knight." She shook her head. He didn't realize he had made a death wish with Satan.

Chapter 30
Manhattan, NY

Mita hated early morning traffic in the city, but this was her everyday life.

She felt really tired this morning and to make shit worse, her period came on yesterday so she was grumpy.

Since the warrants for Money's and Troy's arrest went out, she had been able to sleep a little better, but when they got put behind bars she would be able to sleep like a baby. Every day she thought about her father's death because he did a good job raising her, so she never forgot that.

Mita needed her morning coffee, so she got off at the next exit, seeing a Dunkin Donuts to her left. She pulled into the drive thru, looking at the menu before ordering.

"I'll have an espresso, please, and two glazed donuts," Mita said into the intercom.

"Okay, just pull up," the woman said from the intercom.

"Thank you," said Mita.

Mita was thinking about the one man she couldn't get out her head, and that was Knight. She had never shared the feeling she shared with Knight with any other male on Earth. Two weeks ago she tried to call him, but his number must have been recently changed. She remembered when she used to visit him in VA and the vibes they shared.

Mita's mind got so caught up in thoughts of Knight that she didn't even see the young woman holding a Dunkin Donuts bag and a cup full of coffee.

"Sorry." Mita laughed because the young woman had caught her zoning out. Mita reached in her purse to get a $20 bill when she heard a scream.

Mita looked up into her rearview mirror because she heard the screams coming from behind her. She saw Money coming her way with a gun.

Boom! Boom! Boom! Boom!

The young Dunkin Donuts worker caught two slugs to the face, killing her. Her body flipped out the drive-through window.

Mita's back window shattered, making her duck and rush to put the car in drive. She flew out of the lot doing 70 miles per hour, getting away from the bullets Money was licking off in her direction

When the Benz made it out, Money jumped on his GXR 100 motorcycle. Money knew that Monday through Friday Mita always stopped at this Dunkin Donuts to get coffee, so he waited until today to bust his move.

When Money found out Mita was the daughter of Judge Santana, he knew he fucked up. Fats didn't even tell him until he found out he had a warrant for his arrest. Money didn't like the fact that Fats didn't even put him up on game before he did the hit. Now he and Troy were wanted for killing a judge.

He knew killing Mita would make it easier, but she moved too much, so it was a little hard to get her where he wanted.

***

Long Island, NY

Fats, Don, and Fats's plug Gotti were in a sports bar watching the NBA game.

"We got a lot of history, Don," Gotti said, coming up from VA.

"I know." Don kept his words short because he hated Gotti. He lost a lot of good men in VA to the wars Gotti's people caused. Looking at Gotti made him think of his dead homies Cap, Pookie, Tank Brim, Lil Two, and his boys who lost their life in the crossfire.

"I'm glad you two can patch old shit up so we can put all our focus on Knight and his crew," Fats said, drinking a beer

"I can send some people up here to get the job done," Gotti said, feeling like Fats couldn't handle Knight and his crew.

"No offense, Gotti, but here in New York we can handle our own, and this is my city," Fats stated strongly, putting on a show for Don because truth be told, he knew he needed more help.

"No disrespect taken. I just want him dead. Have you ever found out who his connect is?" Gotti asked, peeping Don's iced grill on the low.

"I haven't, but I'm trying," Fats lied. He had never even tried to find out anything about the connect's identity.

"Well, he moving a lot of shit up here. I'm hearing about him in VA, but what I'm trying to say is he must be dealing with someone very heavy," Gotti stated.

"I agree. To lock down the Bronx, you need a lot of shit," Don agreed with Gotti.

"Who is heavier than us on the East Coast?" Fats asked with a chuckle, feeling himself.

"Maybe he got a plug out in the West Coast or down south," Don said.

"I ain't thinking about that. I'm going to make some calls and see if I can hear something, fam," Fats said.

"I'ma do the same thing." Gotti knew Knight had to be plugged into someone more powerful than him or on the same level.

"Facts." Don nodded his head because he wanted Knight dead. He hated it had to come to this, but Don knew in the game, you could never get too close to people.

"I have to catch my flight back home with your load. It should be here in New York soon. Don, nice having a sit-down with you. Everything is behind me, and I hope vice versa the same is true." Gotti looked Don in his eyes for the truth, but saw none.

"Of course. Take care," Don said as Gotti walked out with his goons out front.

"I'ma kill that nigga one day," Fats said.

"I can't tell, the way you was just sucking him off," Don said.

"It's the game," Fats said before getting up to leave.

Chapter 31
Upper West Side, NY

India had been leasing a nice penthouse in a skyrise for the past few months.

Things with Paco had been getting very serious and intense. He told her about his three-way relationship and she told him being number four would be her pleasure.

India felt Paco's tongue trace her little pussy, which sent electric shocks through her body.

"Ohhh shit," she moaned, leaning her head all the way back, breathing hard and shallow.

When Paco came to her crib, she answered the door naked, showing her sexy body. They wasted no time as they began kissing and touching each other and moving to the bedroom. Moments later, India was on the bed on her back with her toes pointed to the ceiling.

She sat up slightly as he sucked on her tiny clit, making her orgasm build inside of her.

"Paco, I'm cumminggg!" she cried as her legs opened wider and her body squirmed.

After the juices flowed from her coochie, she went for his pole to tease him. India sucked the tip, making him moan as she swallowed his entire cock.

"Damn, India." Paco saw her do magic tricks on the pole.

India tightened her lips and popped her head up and down with intensity and speed, feeling pre-cum slowly fill her mouth. She continued to take him into the back of her throat until Paco shot a thick heavy load down her throat.

"Fuck me now, daddy," she said with her sexy eyes.

"I'm a cuff you up." Paco pulled out a pair of metal furry cuffs for her.

"I never used cuffs before." India smiled, ready to get freaky.

"Close your eyes," Paco told her as he put her hands behind her head and cuffed her up.

"Fuck me good." India said it with her eyes closed, still waiting on him to tell her to open up.

Paco stared at her pretty clean-shaven lips.

India felt something metal like a vibrator go in her pussy, but the feeling just didn't seem right. She opened her eyes to see Paco with a serious face and a pistol shoved in her coochie.

India got caught slacking. She didn't even know how to react.

"You going to tell me everything?" Paco said, seeing her shed real tears.

"I had to, Paco. I'm sorry," she said because she really fell for him.

"Too late for your apologies. This ain't no Donell Jones love song, bitch." Paco still had his gun in her privates, feeling her juices leak on his hand and down the gun.

"Uncle Pimp made me and Cassey go after you and your crew after y'all killed his family. Me and Cassey are well-trained, Paco. I could have been killed you, but I enjoyed your company. I can't lie. I was falling for you," she said, being honest.

"Why do you work for him?"

"He has all of us brainwashed. He got me pregnant. He uses my son as a weapon so I'll do what he says," India admitted.

"If I let you go, what will happen?" Paco asked.

"Don't. Please just kill me. I'm worthless. Just save my son for me," India said, smiling.

Paco knew he had to do the right thing.

Bloc! Bloc! Bloc!

Paco shot her in the pussy then twice in her head, leaving her dead on the white sheets slowly turning dark red.

***

Brownsville, BK

Bree had recently seen a nice brownstone apartment she was interested in and contacted the homeowner. She loved her condo, but she wanted something in the hood also.

The Benz G-Wagon truck rolled over the Brooklyn potholes.

"Pull over," Bree told her two goons in the front seat.

"Right here on the corner?" the driver asked, seeing a group of thugs posted up on the corner in front of the store.

"Yep." Bree tucked her gun in her lower back side.

Bree wore white tight Fendi low-cut jeans, Fendi heels, and a fur coat on top of her tank top, showing her stomach.

"You want us to come, boss?" her goons asked.

"For what?" Bree said, climbing out of the truck

Walking to the store, all she heard was "damn" and "wow". She was used to that type of shit.   Bree bought a pack of bubble gum and walked back outside to see the whole block quiet.

"Who runs this joint over here?" she asked the crew.

"I do," a young black brother said, getting off some milk crates.

"How many keys you move in a week?" she asked, blowing and popping gum.

"What?" He laughed at the other niggas.

"Oh, you must be moving grams," she said.

"Who are you, police?" the kid asked now, serious, but he knew she was too sexy to be the police.

"Nah, I'm that bitch that's going to make you rich," she said.

The kid looked at her jewelry, truck, and gear and knew she had to be somebody big.

"Five," he said.

"Take my number. Call me. I got fifty keys for you, 70/ 30 percent." She gave him her number before turning around to see the Hellcat pull up and 50 and Money hop out.

Bree wasted no time in pulling out her weapon and when the goons posted up saw it, they went with her.

Boc! Boc! Boc!

Bree fired rounds at Money as 50 hit three goons with his Drako.

Tat! Tat!

Niggas started to run and get low from the Draco rounds as they caught a couple of people.

Bree and Money went back and forth until the block was almost cleaned. She hopped in her truck and her driver pulled off, leaving her other goon dead in the street.

"Thanks for the help," Bree told her driver, who didn't help.

"That's out of my pay grade," the driver stated.

Later that night, Bree killed her driver, leaving him dead in the truck.

Chapter 32
San Jose, Costa Rica

Getting off the private flight looking like a true diva, Julie took off her designer shades looking at one of the most delightful cities she ever saw. As she had come in on the private jet, the crystal ocean water and the beautiful tropical private island made she wish she lived here.

Four vans waited for her arrival on the ground.

The tropical climate in the dry season made her want to stay for vacation. But Julie wasn't here on vacation more business. Julie had come out to Costa Rica to meet with her plug Anna, who was a queenpin. She was the biggest operation in Central America.

She got in the first van with men dressed in black cargo outfits with assault rifles. They whispered something in Spanish, saying how they would like to eat her ass, then laughed as they pulled off. Julie laughed because obviously they had no clue she was at Latina woman. Julie told him in Spanish that eating her ass would be the only thing they would be able to do because they were too small for any pleasure. The soldiers were now on fire as they drove through the capital of Costa Rica.

Julie loved the banana trees and palm trees everywhere. They gave the city a foreign vibe.

As they drove past the San Juan River and the tip of Culero Island, she started to think about Knight. Dealing with a man like Knight she knew would bring her billions because New York was a gold mine.

After the twenty minute ride, the van pulled into a lush landscape with long entries wrapped around a driveway with a two-story entrance. The eighteenth century stone mansion was a beauty. Julie always got a little jealous when she saw it. Julie had been dealing with Anna for a while now since leaving California.

Anna's guards let her inside and the first thing she saw was a waterfall in the middle of the lobby.

"Is that Julie?" a beautiful Latina woman said, coming out from the back in an expensive outfit and wearing a lot of jewelry. The woman was Anna.

Anna was in her early thirties, mid-height, perfect body, long blonde hair, bright eyes, and her skin complexion was white as mestizo, as most Latinos would say.

"Look at you," Julie said, hugging Anna.

The women had a stronger bond than just business because their grandparents used to do business before they were even born.

"You made it right on time for dinner. How was your flight and the ride over here?" Anna asked, walking down a long hallway leading to her backyard.

"It was okay, but them goons got foul mouths on them." Julius shook her head, thinking about their comments.

"Okay. They will be dead before you leave," Anna said, smiling, but she was serious.

Once outside, Julie saw a man sitting at a table tied up to a chair with a rope in his mouth, making him unable to talk.

"What's this?" Julie asked.

"Oh, I'm sorry, you caught me in the middle of something. I didn't expect you until later. But since you here, let's eat," Anna said, looking at all the food covering the table.

Anna had personal cooks and maids. She even had an outside kitchen with a hot tub, pool, and a patio large enough to throw parties.

"He's joining us?" Julie saw the old man stare at her. The old man looked as if he was somebody heavy from his expensive attire.

"This is the leader of the top cartel family in Nicaragua, a very dangerous man, but my sister recently took over his empire three hours ago," Anna said, looking at her expensive watch.

"I haven't seen Helena in a long time." Julie liked Helena. She was down to earth, but crazy.

Anna picked up the gun off the table next to the roasted pig. Anna shot the man four times in his face, killing him with no type of remorse.

"So what's up with them American boys?" Anna asked, sitting down so they could start eating.

"I'm single."

"Why?" Anna asked, grabbing a plate, filling it with rice, pork, and stew.

"I got my own bullshit I deal with. I don't have time to stress over a piece of shit." Julie's words were from her heart. She knew her worth as a woman.

"I found an American, and oh my God! Anna said, laughing.

"Tell me?" Julie was happy for her.

"Not yet, mami. I just want to make sure he's the one. But he is definitely a piece to the chessboard," Anna told her before changing subjects to business.

Julie's drugs were already waiting for her in Miami. Anna was on point when it came to business.

Chapter 33
Spring Lake, New Jersey

The Chrysler minivan creeped through the streets in the upscale neighborhood in Jersey. Paco, Knight, and Kazzy all listened to the G Herbo mixtape, loading up their assault rifles.

Today had been long awaited for by Paco and Kazzy since Uncle Pimp sent India and Cassey to them.

"Yo, Kazzy, you sure you can trust that Cassey chick?" Knight asked, driving to the address Paco gave him.

"Yes." Kazzy didn't feel like explaining himself because he felt a connection with Cassey and he knew they wouldn't understand.

"I hope so, nigga, because I'm ready to murk anything that's a part of him," Paco said, putting on his grade three bulletproof vest.

"Everything must go. Leave no witnesses, but we have to find them two little kids – India's son and Cassey's little sister," Paco said, watching Kazzy picking up a submachine gun 2000 and folding it in half while Knight and Paco both pick up their MP4s.

* * *

Uncle Pimp laid on his living room couch surrounded by six beautiful women. This was Uncle Pimp's second mansion in Jersey. His other spot had the rest of the girls training the new recruits.

The NBA game on his large flat screen had all of his attention as he yelled and screamed at the TV.

"Sorry-ass Nets!" he said.

"What happened, daddy?" a short thick Egyptian chick stated, wrapping her leg around his.

"Bitch, did I tell you to talk?" Uncle Pimp had trained his slaves to only speak when spoken to, something he learned from his mentor. Uncle Pimp's mentor was an older man named OG Wise. He taught the young pimp the game at an early age. OG Wise now lived in Dominican Republic like a true boss.

The recent news of India's body being found and Cassey going missing made him nervous and uncomfortable. He knew India was a stand-up bitch and would not fold, but Cassey was a different story.

Cassey's little sister was seventeen and starting to blossom. He had big plans for her.

Uncle Pimp had other homes where he held his sex slaves captive, so this place was just one of many.

"I'm going to sleep. Apple and Honey, yeah, put daddy to bed." Uncle Pimp got up and two women with guns followed him into the hallway, going upstairs.

Before making it to the top flight, the front door got kicked in and landed on the Brazilian cherry wood floor. Apple and Honey were the first to shoot because the gunmen didn't see them on the stairs.

Boc! Boc! Boc!

Paco dodged a bullet from the golden-complexioned chick wearing nothing but a thong.

Tat! Tat! Tat! Tat!

Paco hit Apple twice in her chest and her body collapsed into the wall before rolling down the stairs.

Uncle Pimp ran off into the hallway upstairs while Honey and Kazzy went back and forth until two wild bullets landed in her head.

"I'm going up top," Knight told his crew when he saw Honey's frail body drop.

"A'ight," Paco replied, walking down the hallway towards the living room with Kazzy on the first floor.

Before either man could even bend the corner, shots rang out from four MP5's assault rifles.

"Shit, boy, it's a gang of naked bitches in there with some big shit," Kazzy said with his back on the wall, not trying to die tonight.

Uncle Pimp's whores were all prepared for things like this and most of them were street bitches anyway.

"You see that?" Paco said, looking at the light switch that controlled the living room light.

"I go left, you go right?" Kazzy asked before hitting a light switch, rolling on the ground into the living room and firing around like a madman as Paco did the same thing.

All four women died in a matter of seconds.

***

Knight slowly opened the door of the room Uncle Pimp had gone into. Knight froze when he saw Uncle Pimp with a gun pointed at the head of the son he had with India. There was a pretty teenage girl in the corner, shaking in tears and fear.

"Go downstairs," Knight told a little girl who looked high as a kite. She almost fell over trying to get up in her pajamas.

"You must be Knight, I assume?" Uncle Pimp asked, backing up to a closet door as the baby cried.

"Put the baby down, coward. I'm the one you want."

"I'm honored, but you obviously don't know what's going on, I see." Uncle Pimp's look said it all.

"Fuck all the game!" Knight shouted.

"I will see you again," Uncle Pimp said, opening the door before tossing the baby in the air towards Knight while shooting the baby twice.

Uncle took off into the closet as Knight caught the baby. Knight put the baby on the ground and ran into the door, which didn't lead to a closet. Instead, there was another vaulted metal door leading into a panic room.

The panic room had a private elevator going to the basement, which led to the streets. The secret pathway had been built years ago.

Uncle Pimp knew Knight was coming. He just didn't know when.

133

Chapter 34
Uptown, Bronx

Cassey and her little sister Allure sat in the living room and watched TV, happy to be back in each other's presence. Allure was a beautiful young woman. She was full blooded Haitian and the spitting image of Cassey.   For the past few days, Cassey had Allure locked in a room in the apartment her and Kazzy stayed at. Cassey wanted to let her sixteen-year-old sister detox all the dope Uncle Pimp put in her. Uncle Pimp drugged all his women so he could easily brainwash them. Cassey knew this because she used to be one of those girls.

"Did he ever touch you?" Cassey had been wanting to ask this, but she wanted to ask at the right time. One thing she knew being around Uncle Pimp so long was that he wouldn't normally touch a young girl until she hit the age of seventeen. Allure's birthday was in a few weeks so she hoped Allure still had her virginity.

"He didn't. He told me I had a few more weeks before I became his slave." Allure's voice was sad.

"You never have to worry about him again, I swear," Cassey told her before tearing up.

"I know. Thank you."

The sisters talked for a few hours and then went to sleep on the living room floor.

Kazzy came back home and placed blankets over both of them because it was cold. He was glad they saved Allure, but India's son didn't make it. Their blocks in the Bronx had been getting raided for a week straight by the police and everybody was getting upset. Kazzy hadn't slept well in weeks, so he laid down and dozed off.

***

Soho, NY

Bree waited in the European five star restaurant for her guests for the evening with Knight. This would be her first sit-down with the man who was heavy all over New York City. She wanted to thank him for his crew help because Official was keeping her posted on the streets. Money's crews had been decreasing and getting killed left and right. Some of Money's crew had been warring with Official's workers in Brooklyn, and Official's crew was going hard.

Bree was looking at a menu with her crew was outside on standby.   She looked up to see a sexy man with dreads and a diamond grill and gray designer Dior for men suit.

"You Bree?" Knight asked, looking at her features, impressed with what he saw.

"Yes, how are you, Knight? Have a seat please." Bree didn't know the man, but he looked like some shit out of a *GQ* magazine.

"It's nice to meet you. I've heard a lot of good things about you and for such a beautiful woman as yourself to be doing the things you do, I respect it," Knight said.

"Ohhh, thank you, and likewise. Your name speaks for itself but your crew has been a big help to my people," she stated.

"Facts. We have the same problems. But how did you get into it with that and his crew I don't understand," Knight wondered.

"Let's order food, because this is going to take a while," she repeated, calling over their waiter. Once the food was brought, Bree began her story. "I'm from VA. That's my hometown. When I was young, I was dealing with an old man named Rick. He was a big trick when I was seventeen. Rick paid me a lot of money to make his son Rich, who moved to VA, fall in love with me, so I did. Rich became a drug lord in VA overnight until he got booked and went to prison for life. While Rich was in prison, me and his brother Big Boi robbed him of everything." Bree stopped to take a bite of her food.

"Damn. Snaky," Knight said.

"Being a snake will get you a long way. But let me finish. Rich finds out he got a son and tries to send his son after me and Big Boi, but I peeped it. Sadly, Big Boi didn't and got killed. Rich's son Don turned up the streets, but when he found out Rich was setting him up to the Feds, shit went left. Don went to prison and killed his father," Bree told the story, shaking her head.

"Don was my celly in prison," Knight said.

"Oh, in New York?" she asked.

"Nah, in VA."

"You were in VA?" Bree asked, having no clue.

"Yeah, I had a little run out there until I got hit with a plug named Gotti," he stated.

"Gotti? Wow do you know that's Fats's connect? I just found out."

"I know now. Small world."

"Hell yeah. Anyway, Don beat the body and came home to a new beef with his brother Bloody, who killed his mom. Don came to New York for answers and by that time I was back with my husband Rick. Long story short, Don got locked up for two bodies and I killed Rick, his grandfather, and took over Brooklyn. Now that Don's home he's with Fats and he really has no clue what he is up against because Fats is the king of the snakes." she took a break to eat her food.

"Wow, this shit crazy!" Knight couldn't believe how everybody was somehow connected to each other.

Knight and Bree kicked it for another hour before parting ways.

Chapter 35
Manhattan, NY

Like K and Red drove on their way to her doctor's appointment.

"How you feel, ma?" Lil K asked as he pulled into a parking garage across the street from Red doctor's office.

"I'm good, why do you ask?" she shot back, looking at civilians walking up and down the streets.

"Just checking on you. You ready to go to Jumah service after your appointment?" Lil K asked, parking.

"Inshallah," she replied.

The couple had been spending a lot of time practicing their Islamic religion.

Lil K hadn't seen his brothers in weeks because he was focused on Red. He missed the streets, but he knew Red needed him. Some days Red would be normal then the next day she would be off, but the doctor said this was normal. Lil K realized the only time she was her regular self was before, during, or after killing people. Red would ask him daily when they would be able to go play, which was a code name for killing. Lil K always told her soon and would see a wicked smile appear on her face.

They walked into the tall building and took the elevator to the sixth floor. Lil K and Red waited in a small office with two other people waiting to be seen. When the doctor came out front, he asked Red to come to the back for her weekly check up on her mental process. Lil K would normally wait outside for Red to come out then leave.

"How are you doing today?" the doctor stated, getting no reply as always because Red didn't talk. Whenever Red came to see her doctor she remained silent, making it very hard for him to do his job.

"How's everything going?" the doctor asked, writing shit down, basically saying she was the same, no progress.

Red looked at him as he continued to ask the same questions he always asked.

"Okay, you make my job so easy, you fucking dummy," the doctor mumbled loud enough so she could hear.

When the doctor logged into his computer, Red swiftly grabbed a pair of big metal scissors from the desk. By the time the doctor realized what was going on, Red had slammed the scissors into his neck repeatedly until blood squirted all over the desk and computer. Red had a big bright smile on her before wiping the blood off the scissors with his coat. She closed the office door after walking out, acting normal.

"Are you ready?" Lil K asked, seeing her in good spirits.

"Yeah. Let's go get something to eat," she stated, walking out of the office.

Lil K felt something off about her energy, but she seemed happy so that was all that mattered.

Once downstairs in the lobby, they saw security all rushing upstairs.

"Damn, I wonder what happened," Lil K mumbled to nobody in particular.

"Who knows, babe?" Red said as they crossed the street, making their way to the car.

***

SoHo, NY

Mita was on her lunch break at a nice hotel, bending over doggy style. When Don entered her tightness from the back, her body tensed up.

"Ummmmm," she moaned, feeling the tip open her sex walls.

Don slowly picked up the speed as he entered her more and more with no condom because her cat was too good to take away the full effect.

"Yes, fuck me!" she cried, holding on to the side of the bed as he grabbed her broad shoulders, going to work. "Oh my God, faster!" she yelled as she started throwing her ass back hard on his pole.

She released herself twice in less than five minutes of getting fucked from the back. Mita knew how to move and roll her hips in a circular motion so she could feel all of him.

Don pounded faster while slapping her ass cheeks, making her go crazy and climax again.

Mita wanted to taste him so she waited until he pulled out to put his rod in her mouth, sucking on the tip then the balls going back and forth. She used both hands while giving him fast sloppy head.

"What the fuck? I'm cumming again, catch it," Don said as Mita let him bust in her mouth.

When they got done, he went his way and she went hers.

Chapter 36
Downtown Brooklyn, NY

Uncle Pimp and four of his females drove up to Brooklyn in a Hummer truck to meet up with Fats. The two bosses had a history with each other, but it wasn't nothing to the point where they couldn't talk about it as men.   In recent months, Uncle Pimp had been feeling like Knight and his crew had been trying to ruin his life. For years he sold drugs in certain parts of New Jersey and all his women brought him millions, so he had no ties to the New York drug game. He couldn't figure out why this Knight kid wanted him so bad because he never crossed paths with him until now.

Next week he had to fly out to Africa to meet with his plug Khalid, who was also his brother. The brothers had more of a business relationship than a brotherly love relationship.

Uncle Pimp pulled up to the strip where Fats agreed to meet him at. When Uncle Pimp and his four bad bitches walked into the strip club, everybody's necks turned, staring at the four sexy women. Even the dancers felt a sense of insecurity as they stared at the women.

Fats waited in the back area with a big gallon of Henny and seven guards. One of them was 50.

"What's up, Pimp?" Fats said, seeing Uncle Pimp walk in the spot in his big shiny Salvatore Ferragamo suit.

"Y'all hoes enjoy yourself," Uncle Pimp told his female shooters, dismissing them.

"Long time, no see. Would you like a drink?" Fats offered.

"Nah, I'm here on business. I've been having a serious problem with a kid named Knight."

"Join the club. You and the rest of New York wants him," Fats said loudly enough to where 50 heard him and laughed.

"So it's clear you're not doing the job correctly." Uncle Pimp saw Fats's face flip flop upside down.

"Nigga, you don't know shit. I got men out here dying in these streets going to war with the Bronx and BK niggas, son. While you in your mansion getting a manicure and your toes painted, we in the field, so next time come correct when you come, fam," Fats said, out of breath.

"Okay, I just came to see if you could help, but I guess not. It looks like he got you shook too." Uncle Pimp stood up to leave, not trying to go back and forth.

"Knight wants you, he going to get you, Pimp," Fats said with an evil smirk.

"May the best man survive," were Uncle Pimp's last words before leaving the club with his clique.

***

Manhattan, NY

Mita had taken off work because she wasn't feeling well. The feeling wasn't a common cold. It was more so her vaginal area. She had been in a local Manhattan clinic since 7 a.m. She had seen the doctor and now she was just waiting on the test results.

Things at work were going fine. She had been having so much work she hasn't had time to look at this Fat person who has been ringing loudly in the DEA and federal offices.

Money and Troy were now on the FBI's Most Wanted list and she couldn't wait until they got caught so her father could rest in real peace and so could she.

The doctor came back into the room with some papers and several medical instruments in his hand.

"Thanks, Doc I knew it was nothing serious, probably a little rash," she said, grabbing her purse to leave.

"Not so fast. I hate to be the bearer of bad news, but you have contracted two sexually transmitted diseases," the doctor said as Mita's eyes got watery.

"Me?"

"Yes, you, Mita, but luckily these diseases are highly curable with antibiotics. You have chlamydia and gonorrhea. The word they use on the street is you're burning. I wrote a couple of prescriptions for you to pick up from CVS, Walgreens, or Rite Aid that will help you get better, but please use condoms. It's a crazy world these days," the doc said before leaving.

Mita couldn't believe she had two STDs. The only person she had been having sex with was Don. She felt like shit. All she could do was go home and cry herself to sleep.

Later that night when she woke up, something hit her. Mita really didn't know Don's background. She fell for him because of his looks and she didn't know him as well as she thought, obviously. Mita spent all night trying to find his real name and nickname and her database.

When Don's photo and name came up, she couldn't believe it. She also peeped the connection between Don's father and Fats. She wondered if her life was at risk and if Don already knew who she was. Looking deeper, she realized her dad was Don's judge and Miller, her ex co-worker, was his DEA, and now they were both dead.

Romell Tukes

Chapter 37
Bed-Stuy, BK

Bones and two of his little cousins walked to the liquor store on Throop Avenue off of Martla Avenue.

The city had been crazy for the past few weeks against Money's crew and Official's and Bones's peoples. Two nights ago a cop got killed and one got shot during a big shootout on J Street near the Supreme Courthouse.

"Yo, Bones, we going to Acers tonight, cuz I heard that shit going to be litty, bro," Bones's cousin 2K stated, grabbing a few bottles from the shelf.

"Where you hear that shit at?" Bones didn't feel like clubbing, but he hadn't been out in months since he and Official hit up a club in Philly.

"My little side bitch works in there," 2K shot back.

"Who is that big tall bitch who looks like a man?" 2K's brother said, pulling out a stolen credit card to swipe the bottles.

***

Money saw Bones's Cadillac SUV parked in front of a liquor store as he drove by on his way to one of his hideouts.

The Feds were in town so he was trying to lay low, but that was hard when he was in the middle of a war with Official guys.

He parked in front of the Crown Chicken fast-food spot next door to the liquor spot. Money grabbed his Glock with an extended clip and said a silent prayer.

When Bones came out laughing with two young boys, he hopped out with his hoodie covering his forehead and eyes.

Boc! Boc! Boc! Boc!

2K's head got blown off and then Bones took cover, dropping his bottles, getting his weapon out. 2K's brother tried to run across the street, almost getting hit by a car, but when two bullets struck his back, he fell to the ground

Bones ducked Money's bullets as he tried to get his Ruger handgun to work, but it wasn't working. When Money saw this, he took advantage and ran down on Bones.

"Fuck," Bones said, seeing Money in front of him with a gun to his face.

"Night-night."

Boc! Boc! Boc! Boc!

Money ran back to his car, racing up the block, taking Bones off his top five hit list in his mind.

***

Uptown, Bronx

Cassey had just come back from food shopping while Kazzy went out to handle some business.

Having her little sister around was great. Everything was going so good Cassey felt like she was living in a fairy tale.

Today she had made plans to take Allure out to a spa and then shopping for some designer fly shit. They'd been talking about getting Allure in school so she could get education because Haiti's school system growing up was one of the worst in the world,

Cassey really appreciated all the help Kazzy had given to her. The thought of marrying him popped in her head every time they had sex or vibed

Walking inside the apartment, she would normally see Allure sitting on the couch watching the *Wendy Williams Show* or *Jerry Springer.*

"Allure!" she yelled, placing the food bags in the kitchen and hoping her sister was dressed so they could go out.

Cassey walked to the back. She looked in the bathroom to see if Allure was in there. "Allure?" Cassey walked into a little room to see her on the floor with the needle in her arm, passed out.

"Noooo!" Cassey screamed. She figured Allure overdosed because of the white foam dripping down her face.

Cassey called 911 crying and screaming, checking for a pulse on her sister's neck, but she couldn't find one.

She had tried so hard to keep her clean, but she knew how hard it is to kick a heroin addiction because she had been there before.

"Allure, noooo, please wake up!" she cried, rocking her little sister and her arms.

When the medical team arrived, they could not do anything to bring her back to life. She was already dead.

Allure had stolen money out of Cassey's purse and went to cop from up the block thirty minutes ago.

Romell Tukes

Chapter 38
Harara, Zimbabwe

Khalid and Uncle Pimp sat in his lush living room staring at each other. They were brothers and businessmen, but they had a strong dislike in for each other.

"Is everything okay with the drugs?" Khalid spoke the first word since Uncle Pimp arrived five minutes ago.

"Yes," Uncle Pimp stated.

"So what the fuck do you want? Why are you here?" Khalid's accent was stern and strong.

"I'm having an issue with a man who I believe is plugged in with you."

"Well, if that's the case, my business is not your business, so I can't help you." Khalid was ready to let him out before he tried to brainwash his wife or children.

Khalid hated pimps. That was one reason he hated his own brother. "His name is Knight."

Now he had Khalid's undivided attention. "What about Knight?" Khalid's blood boiled.

"He killed my family and my women," Uncle Pimp said.

"I don't care about your family or whores. Where can I find Knight?" Khalid shouted.

"My people are searching, but he is not a dummy. It's going to take time."

"Find him before I do, because if I have to come to the States, I will spare no soul," Khalid said, getting up to leave.

Uncle Pimp left Khalid's castle and made his way to the airport, coming up with a plan of his own.

***

South Miami, FL

Julie and her crew of armed guards entered the large glass mansion to meet with a Cuban boss. The Cuban boss Sisqo was her client and close peer. She walked into the large kitchen, leaving her men out front in the hallway with Sisqo's guards.

"Julie, you look so beautiful," Sisqo stated, getting up in his silk robe to hug her as he always did.

"Sisqo, cut the nice talk, papi. What is it? You never call me." Julie sat down on a stool, looking at him. She knew Sisqo like the back of her hand.

"I'm having a little problem," he said with his head down.

"I'm on my period. I have a bigger problem. Now spit it out, damn!" she shouted, getting impatient.

"Someone is trying to take over my turf and I am losing a lot of men and money. When I lose money, so do you," he said.

"Wow. You're a grown-ass man. This is your problem. We cool and shit, but I'm a businesswoman." Julie knew Sisqo had to be smoking or sniffing his product if he thought she was about to get in his turf war. She was the plug.

"You don't see the big picture. Stephen is trying to take over the city."

When he said Stephen, she listened. "That bitch? I thought she left the city?" Julie hated Stephen. She was her only competition and they were neck to neck in the drug game.

"I got my men on her, but she was too powerful. She sends my men back in pieces every time," he said, knowing beefing with Stephen was a death wish.

"Don't worry about it. Keep doing what it is you do."

Julie left with hatred in her heart and eyes for Stephen.

Chapter 39
Manhattan, NY

Mita got a surprise call from Knight last night and they both agreed to meet up at an ice skating rink on the beautiful but chilly Sunday. Her STD's were both gone now so she was back to her normal self.

She watched the little kids have fun on the ice rink with their family and friends. Mita started to think back to when she was a little girl, with our father and how they used to come to the same place. When she saw Knight coming her way, she couldn't help but smile at his presence.

"Hey, what's up, stranger?" Mita said, gave him a hug.

"You smell good. I see you got your blades on," Knight stated looking down at her skates.

"Before we skate, I just want to talk to you." Mita grabbed his hand to sit down.

"What's the vibes, big head?" he joked.

"A lot of shit changed since I used to come visit you prison," she said, crossing her legs.

"I see," he said, looking at her thick thighs.

"I'm serious," she replied

"What's on your mind, Mita?"

"I know who you are under this person I see," she said.

"Who I am?" He wondered where she was going with this.

"You're Knight, and you run one of the biggest drug rings in New York. And if you don't know, I'm the head district attorney in the city." Her words hit him hard.

"Why tell me now?" he asked her, looking around to see if police were going to come out from everywhere.

"I had to create a distance and guard myself because by the time I found out who you really were, I was already in love with you." Mita couldn't believe she just put everything on the table.

"What does this mean?"

"Nothing at all. I just felt like I should let you know what I am on and you're okay with me"

"So, can I get you on the payroll?"

"Don't push it. I will put you in cuffs," she joked with him.

"Let's skate, then go grab a bite to eat. I'm starving." Knight got up and took her hand to go skating.

After an hour of skating and having fun with each other, the two turned in their ice skates.

"That was fun," Knight told her.

"I feel like I just exercised for a whole hour." Mita laughed, feeling sore and her lower body section.

"Facts." Knight held her warm hand in the parking lot.

"Where are we going to eat? Because I know a good spot in Hell's Kitchen," Mita said.

Knight saw a glimpse of a shadow appear between two cars. Knight slid in front of Mita and reached for his gun, but Money beat him to the punch.

Boc! Boc! Boc!

Mita yelled once she saw Knight get hit in the upper left arm.

Bloc! Bloc!

Knight fired back at Money, hitting him in his right hand, making him drop his weapon. Knight thought he had the upper hand and could have killed Money, but he heard Mita call his name.

Money took off through the parking lot, bleeding from his hand.

"Oh my God, you saved my life and yours!" Mita saw a gash on his left arm.

"We have to leave."

"Do you know him?" Mita asked, walking to their cars.

"Some things you don't ask a gangster," Knight told her.

***

"Drive, son!" Money shouted, jumping in the getaway car 50 was driving.

"Did you get her?" 50 asked.

"Nah. You not going to believe who I just saw with her?" Money had come to kill Mita. He tailed her for hours. He saw a man with the hoodie skating with her, but he had no clue it was Knight.

"Who?" 50 said turn it on to a highway leading back to Brooklyn.

"Knight."

"Oh shit, what the fuck he doing with her?"

"He's probably working for them people." Money shrugged.

"Damn, this shit wacked, bruh. Wait until I tell Don," 50 said.

Don was sick when Fats told him a DA bitch named Mita was on his line. He wished he would have killed her.

Romell Tukes

Chapter 40
Queens, NY

Troy was hidden out in Queens with his sister, trying to lay low and avoid Brooklyn. The Feds had him on the FBI's Most Wanted list. He was sick about that, but he knew what came with this gangster hardcore life he lived. He had some money saved up, so he was planning to head to Texas in a few days where his brother lived.

The all-black Acura raced through the streets at full speed. Troy was a real speed demon. He loved to drive fast.

A cop car came out from a side building and put his lights on.

"Fucking bitch!" Troy yelled, as he banged on the steering wheel out of anger.

Troy pulled over as the thought of him taking a cop on a high-speed chase popped in his mind. But he trusted the fake ID in his possession would get him through this encounter.

A young white racist cop got out with a chip on his shoulder and one hand on his gun. "Roll down your fucking window," the cop said, coming up to the window.

"Yes, officer, how may I help you, sir?" Troy asked respectfully.

"You were speeding. And how can you afford this nice car?" the cop asked

"Is this a traffic stop or an interview?" Troy responded.

"ID and license?" the cop asked, seeing Troy reach under his seat. "Aaaahhhh!" the cop yelled.

Boc! Boc! Boc! Boc!

The cop shot Troy four times in his chest, killing him, and then called in for backup. Minutes later, he found out Troy was wanted for murder and he had two loaded pistols under his feet, so the cop was labeled a hero. This was his third time killing a black man this month.

***

Downtown Brooklyn

Official's brother Hector was out with his two sons spending father and son time, something he rarely did because of work. Hector was a road manager for a local rap artist in Brooklyn. His two sons were teenagers in middle school, and his baby mother owned her own business.

He walked out of GameStop with bags full of games for his kids.

"Daddy, are you coming to the house to play Call of Duty?" one of his sons asked, walking across the street.

"No, I can't. I have to go overseas tonight so I have to get ready" Hector stated before two cars pulled up the next to his luxury car.

"You Hector?" Don asked, rolling down his window.

"Yeah, but no business right now. Call my office," Hector said, walking off until he saw the windows go down in the back.

Bloc! Bloc! Bloc! Bloc! Bloc!

A bullet hit Hector in his head and the other bullets killed his two boys.

***

Forty minutes later, Official and his crew were in Kings County Hospital. Official's cousin worked at the hospital and called him when he saw Hector and his two sons rolling in with serious injuries. Official didn't even know his brother was back in town. Normally Hector would hit him up.

There was no doubt that this was someone from Money's crew who did this shit and he had plans to make them pay.

His cousin came out from the back, looking exhausted and drained. "Official, Hector didn't make it. I'm sorry."

"How about the boys?"

"One of them died on the scene and the other one, li'l Mike, is in the ICU so he may make it. He's fighting."

Official was ready to kill but he had to be smart. He knew every dog has his day.

Chapter 41
Downtown Brooklyn

Fats and 50 were on their way to a NBA basketball game at the Barclays Center. A truck full of shooters was a few feet behind him for extra backup.

"The cops killed Troy," Fats said in a nonchalant tone.

"Don told me." 50 shook his head as Cookie laid on his shoulder wearing a fashion Nova outfit.

The truck stopped at a four-way intersection a few blocks away from the destination. Cookie looked out the windows to see three motorcycles pull up to the side of them.

"Babe, look at the fly bitch on the bike. I want one," Cookie said.

50 and Fats looked out the window to see all three bikers lift up machine guns.

Tat! Tat! Tat! Tat! Tat!

Cookie's face and body got riddled with bullets and so did the driver's. 50 and Fats got out of the SUV as a shooter shot up the truck.

The gunmen in the SUV behind them didn't stand a chance as Lil K killed all four of them.

50 and Fats went bullet for bullet with the crew. Fats hid behind a truck while Red jumped off the bike and creeped around the SUV, hitting Fats twice in his stomach.

Lil K, Red, and Paco jumped back on the bikes, leaving 50 helping Fats to stay alive as civilians get out of their cars to call police.

50 saw the cops coming down the block and sneaked off, calling Don to pick him up.

Blood was all over his clothes from Cookie and Fats. He took off his sweater and tossed it into the corner trash.

***

Brooklyn Medical Center

D'Aray went to the hospital when she got the call from her mom saying her sorry-ass father was there. Even though she didn't fuck with Fats, he was still her father so before he died, she felt like it would only be right to show her respect.

Things with her and Paco had been okay since India was out of the picture. She and Jadaya were coming up with a plan to take India out of the picture when she was alive because Paco was paying her too much attention.

D'Aray figured that Fats was on the fifth floor, which was the ICU floor. She knew that because years ago she used to work there.

She took the elevator, texting Paco to tell him where she was, and then she texted Jadaya the same message.

The floor smelled like death. It was cold and so bright it would hurt a person's eyes.

On her way down the hall, the familiar voice calling her name stopped her.

"Jadaya, what are you doing here?"

"What are you doing here? I just got your text," Jadaya stated with puffy eyes and tissue in her hand.

"My father got shot, so I came to check on him." D'Aray's mind started to shift as she looked into the first room to see Fats laying in a hospital bed.

"Me too."

"Can't be," D'Aray mumbled, walking into Fats's room. He was up and watching both women.

"I'm glad both of you came. I'm sorry that I was never the best dad, but I still love all my children regardless."

That caught both of their attention.

"Let me make sure I'm hearing this shit correctly. This is my sister here right here? My girlfriend?" D'Aray asked for a clear understanding just in case she was overlooking shit.   "Your girlfriend?" Fats said, shocked because he had no clue they even knew each other.

"Dad, this is fucked up! I don't even know who you are." Jadaya ran out of the room crying.

D'Aray just stood there, shaking her head. "They should have killed your lowdown ass," D'Aray said before leaving the room to catch up with Jadaya.

She couldn't believe this whole time she'd been having sexual relationships with her sister. She felt nasty.

Fats felt no type of way about it. In his mind he did it for their own good. What he couldn't get out of his head was when D'Aray just said they should have killed him. How did she know it was "they"?

He started to think his daughter has something to do with him being shot and if so, she just made her own casket.

Romell Tukes

Chapter 42
Canon, USP prison, PA
Weeks later

Less came and visited his brother in prison because he knew tomorrow is never promised with his lifestyle.

Things were so crazy in the Bronx and Brooklyn since Fats got hit up. Knight had to shut down shop all throughout the South Bronx area. Two nights ago, Less got into a shootout on the highway on his way home. 50 and Don turned his car into Swiss cheese. He was just happy to get out of that situation.

D Fatal Brim walked out, chewing on a toothpick, smiling at his little brother.

"Damn, son, you got gray hair already." Less laughed, hugging his brother before sitting back down

"Nigga, fuck out of here! I see you putting on weight, fat boy." D Fatal Brim loved to see Less because he was always his favorite brother.

"I'm eating good, fam. But what's up with you?"

"Shit, it is what it is, bro. I'm macking, working on these new laws coming out, trying to get home and sucker duck. These niggas goofy in this bitch."

"I be knowing, blood." Less knew being around niggas all day you would start to see who niggas really were instead of who they pretend to be.

"I'm just trying to get home soon. But what's up with Knight? He sent me some pictures from Miami with some bad bitches from out there."

"He be back and forth out there. I have no clue what he got going on."

"One thing about the bro is he's a mastermind. He always thinks ahead," D Fatal Brim stated seriously. He knew Knight like the back of his hand.

"I remember that day I came out the building and saw both of y'all niggas robbing them three niggas, bro. Y'all had them clowns-ass naked sucking on their thumbs with one leg in the air," Less joked.

"That was your boy Knight's idea. I remember that shit, homie, because the niggas came back and shot up the block. They killed Thin," D Fatal Brim said.

The visit lasted until 2 p.m. and then Less drove back to the Bronx to get up with Paco.

***

Williams Bridge, BX

Lil K walked into his home after building with Less and Paco about sliding out to Brooklyn on a location Fats went to on his chill time. He heard a loud noise coming from the bedroom when he saw a trail of bloodstains on the carpet. Lil K grabbed his SK assault rifle from his closet, thinking Red was in trouble as he creeped to the back room, hearing Red's voice.

"Who you work for, nigga? This the second time I saw you peeping around here. You got five seconds to tell me," Red said, pointing her gun at the man's head as blood leaked down his face.

"Red!" yelled Lil K, snapping her out of whatever zone she had drifted into.

"Hey babe, I thought you were out of town?" she asked nervously, trying to block the victim.

When Lil K saw who it was, he knew Red was tripping hard.

"Why do you have the fucking landlord tied up?" Lil K said, seeing duct tape around a man's mouth, hands, and ankles

"The what?" She looked lost.

"He owns the place." Lil K didn't even want to say more.

"He was creeping around the house for two days. I thought he was the enemy," she said in a kiddie voice

"Pack your shit. We leaving." Lil K looked at the upset landlord, whose face was painted red.

"I'm sorry." Red ran over to pack her bags.

Lil K killed the landlord and helped her pack up the important items so they could move. Luckily he had a fake name on the lease just in case something like this ever happened.

***

JFK Airport, NY

Knight and Kazzy boarded the flight to Miami on a business trip for a night. Kazzy wanted to get out of New York.

Knight wanted Kazzy to meet the plug just in case anything was to go wrong, like jail or death.

Less was out in Brooklyn hunting down Money with Official and his crew.

As soon as Knight got on the plane, he went to sleep something he rarely did, especially with Mita was in his life. She came over to his crib four times a week.

Chapter 43
North Miami Beach, FL

"This must be it, bro," Knight stated, parking on the curb across the street from a lounge, which had Latin men and women coming in and out.

"Damn, they got some bad bitches in this bitch." Kazzy saw all the beautiful women dressed in tight little dresses everywhere.

"Yo, bro, this ain't that type of situation. We here on business, so don't fuck this up," Knight said, knowing how Kazzy liked to think with his dick.

"I ain't worried about these thots. I got Cassey."

"Yeah, but she not here." Knight walked into the bar to see Julie and her army blocking up the whole back section.

"Follow my lead," Knight said, walking up to Julie's linebacker guards.

"Let him in, assholes," Julie said over the loud Spanish music.

"Julie, what's up, ma?" Knight gave her a hug.

When Kazzy saw how bad and sexy the plug was, he almost choked on his spit.

"Who dis?" she asked, looking at Kazzy with a warm smile, which was deadly.

"This is Kazzy, my brother. I told you about him last trip. If anything was to ever happen to me, he will be taking over," Knight repeated.

"Oh yeah, nice to meet you Kazzy. I'm Julie." She extended her hand to him.

"My pleasure," Kazzy replied, taking her hand and kissing it make it blush crazy.

"I gotta to keep an eye on you," she joked as they all sat down.

"I'd love to keep my eye on you," Kazzy shot back while Knight gave him a look to shut the fuck up.

"Be careful what you wish for, Kazzy. I'm a different breed of animal," she said with a smile as six bottles arrived with sparkles.

"Me too," Kazzy said, flirting back, paying Knight no mind.

"How's business?" Knight spoke up before shit got crazy.

"Great. I'll be sending you something this week, right?" she asked.

"Facts," Knight shot back.

"I'm sending a gift for your birthday also." She popped one of the bottles.

"How do you know?" Knight saw a clique walking into the spot and so did Julie.

"What is she doing here? Let her in!" Julie shouted.

"Hey Julie…" Bree paused when she saw Knight and Kazzy there. It really surprised her.

"Hi Bree. What are you doing out here?" Julie asked while pouring Knight and Kazzy a drink.

Bree saw her entertaining Knight and a hint of jealousy entered her veins.

"I'm out here chilling, hitting a few clubs." Bree tried not to make eye contact with Knight, but she couldn't help it. He looked good tonight.

"How rude of me, Bree. This is Knight and his brother Kazzyyyy." Julie dragged out the end of Kazzy's name to let him know she was feeling him.

"I'm aware of the Bronx legends," Bree said.

"What's up, Bree?" Knight stated.

"Ain't shit, just out here vibing. Well, I'm going to let y'all kick it. I was just stopping by," Bree said, turning to leave, wondering how Knight got plugged in with her plug.

"Oh, Bree, your people still owe $375,000. I'm sure you will take care of it, love," Julie said, stunting in front of her guests.

"Yeah, I got you tonight. I'll Cash App it."

Bree was heated. Julie had just played her.

That whole night, Julie and Kazzy enjoyed themselves as if Knight wasn't even there. Kazzy and Julie chemistry filled the room even her goons felt the vibe.

***

Newark, New Jersey

Uncle Pimp had just recruited two young women he met in a club in the hood. He had a routine. He would get down with his new women to break them in and brainwash them. Since his mind wasn't focused on his pimp game, he would have to let his hoes do the job for him.

Knight and his crew were heavy on his mind, especially Cassey with the double cross. He trained his bitches to never cross him and out of all of his hoes, he trained Cassey the best.

Meeting with Khalid in Africa turned out to be a dry run but he was making his own plans to get his Payback.

He drove back to his mansion to see his whores lined up waiting on the new arrivals.

Chapter 44
Canaan USP Prison, PA

"Yo, homie, you got a visit. The police just went to the cell looking for you." CJay started walking in a small room prisoners used to exercise inside.

"A'ight, here, take this, homie," D Fatal Brim stated, pulling out a long sharp knife from his pants.

"Damn, blood, you trying to kill a nigga?" CJay said.

"If shit pop off, a nigga got to go to work," D Fatal Brim said, already dressed.

He was talking to a nigga from D.C. about some money he owed D Fatal Brim for over two months. D.C would try to get over on a New York nigga if they let them.

D Fatal Brim already knew who was coming to see him. He and his girl met on a dating site a while back. A lot of inmates used dating sites to get women to ride with them on their bid.

When he met Maria, he didn't know how she looked until months later and when he saw her, he couldn't believe it. A lot of the women on the prison dating sites were lonely or they seemed to have low self-esteem.

During the visit, D Fatal Brim couldn't stop smiling, sitting across from Maria, who was one of the baddest bitches in the room.

"You look all buff," Maria said, pushing her long jet-black hair behind her ear.

"I worked out before I came down. How was the flight?" he asked.

"Oh my God, daddy, LAX be so crowded there," she stated, licking her lips.

Maria was a beautiful Mexican woman with a lot of money. She found him one day while at a friend's house while looking for one of her ex-boyfriends on a dating site. Since that day she had been in love with him. She had been coming up to visit him sending pictures, letters, books, and money.

"What's been going on in there?" she asked, referring to prison.

"Same old shit, I guess, but when I think about you, call you, or email you, it takes me out of here."

"You're just trying to make me feel good." She smiled, showing her deep dimples.

"I wish I could make you feel real good," he shot back.

"You so nasty! Speaking of nasty, was that sticky shit on the letter you sent me semen?"

"Did you lick it?"

"You know I did," she said, laughing because she really did lick the paper.

***

Albany, NY

Money came back to his city to pay Troy's tombstone a visit. When he got killed by police, his family moved him back to Albany in a body bag to bury him in his hometown.

To some degree, Money felt like it was his fault his right hand was dead at the hands of the police.

The war going on in NYC was getting crazier by the day. Money planned to lay low in his hood since the Feds wanted him and he knew they wouldn't look here.

Seeing Knight with the DA bitch made him realize there was some funny shit going on that he didn't want no parts of.

Chapter 45
East New York, BK

50 rode to make a move for Fats, who wanted him to pick up two million dollars in cash from a nigga named Pay G from Pikni projects. Fats didn't tell 50 that the project people was the most dangerous hood besides the Pink House in the city.

Don had flown out to Virginia for the week to take care of some business down with the crew. 50 and Don had VA on a lock with the dope game right now while in New York and after killing Knight, they planned to go back home.

The project had a few tall buildings. Outside of them were goons posted up in Timbs and Yankees caps.

50 pulled the Ferrari over as niggas stared into the car. Seeing niggas gather up surrounding his car, he got a little nervous so he called the number Fats gave him to reach Pay G.

"Yo, this 50."

"It's good to meet you, little nigga. You came to the wrong city," the male voice stated.

"This Pay G?" 50 asked, looking at the phone as if it was a face.

"Nigga, this Official. Your man Pay G tied up right now, li'l homie. Have fun getting out the hood, little homie," Official said before the phone hung up.

50 saw niggas coming from everywhere with guns. He wasted no time and hit the gas pedal, getting the fuck out of there as bullets hit his car from everywhere. 50 made it down the block without getting killed. His heart was racing. He couldn't believe what just happened. This was some fishy shit. He went straight to Fats's crib to see what was up with that shit because it didn't seem right.

50 had no clue that Pay G was a guest in the BK. When Official got word that the nigga worked for Fats, he kidnapped him.

When Official told the niggas in the projects who killed Bones, they were down for Official because niggas loved Bones in the hood.

Official and his goons killed Pay G and left him on the top of the building with his head chopped off a few feet away from the body.

***

South Miami, FL

Julie and Bree were riding in the backseat of her pink Maybach with a van tailing her full of shooters. The women were going to the beach.

"Why was Knight out here?" Bree asked.

"Excuse me?" Julie thought she heard her wrong.

"I just never knew you had any ties with him," Bree stated.

"You and him have some type of beef or something?" Julie asked, because she didn't have time to get caught up in any beef.

"No, not at all." Bree just wanted to see where Julie's head was at.

"So why are you asking in regards about my personal business?" Julie looked at her.

"I didn't know he was dealing with you." Bree's words came out wrong.

"Pull this bitch over," Julia said to her driver.

"Everything okay?" Bree asked.

"Bitch, emotions and business don't mix and I recently heard you killed your husband for the clout. I don't fuck with snakes. I was just waiting for the right time to cut you off, mami, so you can get out now!"

"What?" Bree thought she was hearing shit.

"Bitch, did I speak Chinese?" Julie grabbed a gold Glock from her purse.

"You got it." Bree got out and Julie pulled off.

Bree couldn't believe what just happened. She felt like killing that bitch. She knew there had to be more as to why her plug cut her off. For the last few weeks, Julie had been acting funny.

Right now, her main worry was finding a plug.

***

Canon USP Prison, PA
One month later

Today was the biggest day of D Fatal Brim's life. He was getting married to his dream girl, Maria. Two weeks ago he asked her to marry him and she happily said yes to him. Now it was the big day.

In the Feds, inmates can only get married at two times during the year and when D Fatal Brim popped the question, the next marriage ceremony was days ago. It only took one day to get a marriage license.

Maria and D Fatal Brim stood face-to-face as the pastor read some verses out of the Bible.

Seeing Maria cry did something to him, he knew Maria was the one he wanted to spend the rest of his life with in jail or in the free world.

Maria bought a home in Long Island so she could be closer to him instead of flying back and forth from Cali to PA every week.

Once married they kissed and hugged tightly, opening a new chapter in life.

Chapter 46
Fulton Avenue, Bronx

At 8:30 a.m., Knight stood in the park's playground area, watching his crew arrive for their meeting. The only thing that was heavy on his mind was the outcome of what he did to call it. He still had bricks from the shit he stole from Khalid and the drugs he was getting from Julie were blowing Khalid's drugs out of the water. Julie's product could be smelled through the wrap and tape, it was so pure.

"Niggas, what's cracking? We was asleep." Kazzy had brought Cassey along because she was the newest member to the crew, and everybody accepted her except Red.

"Good morning, family," Knight said, picking up folders for everyone, passing them out to everybody.

"What is this?" Lil K asked, seeing photos of a few familiar faces.

"Those are all the ops and enemies, bro. Our first target will be Uncle Pimp tomorrow in A.C. at the Trump Casino. Thanks to Cassey, we know he goes there once a year for an annual pimp ball with all the East Coast pimps," Knight said, repeating everything he heard from Cassey.

"Who is sliding out there?" Less asked, looking through the folder.

"Cassey, Kazzy, and Lil K," Knight stated.

"Okay, good!" Cassey cheered.

"What about us? Paco asked, feeling left out.

"You and Red take care of Frenchy Kid, because he is a problem now with a crew of Dominicans."

"Damn, son, I got to stay in Brooklyn with the wild-ass niggas?" Less wasn't feeling that.

"No. I need you to come with me to Chiraq," said Knight.

"Chiraq? Nigga, I'd rather stay in Brooklyn," Less shot back, already knowing how them niggas got down

"Nah, we are not going out there on drill time. This personal," Knight said before leaving the crew.

"I'll meet you two in New Jersey at 10 p.m. tomorrow," Lil K told Kazzy and Cassey, hoping she knew how to use a gun.

***

Atlantic City, NJ

The Trump Casino was filled with pimps from all over the tri-state area. Uncle Pimp and Mac Fly from Philly ran this every year and everybody came out to show love.

"What's up, pimp? I see you down a couple. Normally I see at least thirteen of your best hoes." A pimp named Draw came up to Uncle Pimp in the ballroom they had rented out.

"This is only a portion of the pie, young'un. My hoes flow like water on the Nile River while yours are obviously a needle in a hay-stack." Uncle Pimp looked at Draw's two busted hoes. They had corns on their feet from walking the streets.

"You got it, Slim," Draw said in his D.C. accent, laughing and walking off.

"Where is my phone?" Uncle Pimp asked one of his hoes.

"I left it in the car," one of the women said.

Everybody at the round table looked at her, knowing she would have to do a punishment later. Uncle Pimp's punishments were crazy and overboard. He made a bitch deep throat horse dick. There was a time he made a bitch stick a baseball bat up her ass.

"Get up, all of you." Uncle Pimp and six of his women got up, moving through the crowds of people.

Outside, Uncle Pimp stopped.

"You crawl through the lot in circles, little bitch." Uncle Pimp grabbed the woman that had left his phone in the car and tossed her on the ground.

Uncle Pimp walked inside the ballroom laughing, respecting the OG's style.

"Let's go to the limo." When Uncle Pimp walked deeper into the lot, Cassey popped out in all black with a gun.

"You bitch! Kill that bitch!" Uncle Pimp yelled, and all his women reached for their guns, but nobody saw Lil K and Kazzy hop out blasting.

Bloc! Bloc! Bloc! Bloc!

Two of Uncle Pimp's women got smoked. Uncle Pimp busted two shots at Cassey after she hit him in his hip bone, making him run for cover.

Boc! Boc! Boc!

Kazzy almost got caught slipping until Cassey popped up and shot two of the women with head wraps. One of the women had a gun to Lil K's head and Cassey fired three shots past Lil K into the head of the woman she knew very well.

Uncle Pimp was crawling under cars until he was a good distance away and then he ran onto the highway limping.

When Kazzy saw this, he knew the sucker got away.

Cassey and Lil K saw the woman crawling on her knees. Lil K was shocked, but Cassey wasn't. Lil K lifted his gun to kill the lady.

"No. She is no older than eighteen. Let her be." Cassey lowered her gun.

They left the crime scene and went back to the Bronx.

Chapter 47
Uptown, Bronx

Frenchy Kid and his childhood friend CEO rode in the new drop top Rolls Royce he had recently copped to show off, letting the city know he was on top. It was almost midnight and he had just left the club. He was on his way to the crib of some chick he had just met hours ago.

Since 50 was supplying him, he was able to feed his crew, which got thicker by the day. He only had one worry, and that was every hustler on the Bronx Road, Knight's crew. If a nigga wasn't down with Knight or his people, then you were fresh fish on the line. It was hard going up against the biggest and most dangerous crew in the whole city.

Stopping at the light, he realized he was in that area. This was like sticking his head in the lion's den or worse, sticking his head in the lion's mouth.

"Yo, Frenchy, who that?" CEO asked, seeing the truck pull up to them. A sexy bitch was waving at them, but they couldn't see the driver.

"I don't know, but she bad. I'm trying to fuck." Frenchy blew her a kiss and directed her to pull over and they both did so.

When the woman jumped out of the truck, they didn't see the Mac 10 submachine gun until she got up on them face to face

Tat! Tat! Tat! Tat! Tat!

She didn't stop shooting until she spread forty-eight rounds into the fancy car, overkilling both men.

Getting back in the car, they pulled off and Red didn't have a care in the world about what she just did.

"You good, Red?" Paco had seen a lot of change in Red since she got shot in the head.

"I'm blessed, Paco. That's your name, right?" Red asked, making sure she had the right person.

***

Downtown Brooklyn

Fats was waiting for Uncle Pimp to arrive at his condo because he had been blowing Fats's phone up for two days straight now.

Hearing the knock at the door made him pull out his gun just in case Pimp had any side thoughts or made any funny movements. Since being shot, Fats was on point, and he was playing for keeps now.

"Let that nigga in!" Fats yelled to his goons.

Uncle Pimp rushed into the apartment upset with a cane.

"What's up?" Fats asked.

"They shot me. I want to kill them, nigga, I swear. They killed all my hoes," Uncle Pimp said with glassy eyes.

Fats couldn't help but laugh so hard he almost fucked up the shit bag he had to carry around for a few more weeks.

"What's so funny?"

"You a scary pimp, not a gangster pimp, nigga. You been running the streets faking," Fats said.

"Look, Fats, I want to help, please! I want them fools dead. I'll pay or whatever," Uncle Pimp cried.

"Slow down. We're gonna get it together."

He and Fats talked for hours trying, to come up with plans for Knight and his crew.

***

Chicago Heights, IL

This was Less's first time in Chicago and he liked what the town had to offer. Last night he met a few BD gang members outside of Harold's Chicken and they clicked after realizing he was from the Big Apple. He made plans to keep in touch with the BD gangsters.

Less was at the hotel asleep while Knight was on his way to handle his business.

***

The cab stopped at a Chuck-E-Cheese and he saw Valentine's car in the parking lot with his beautiful daughter Karmla inside. Knight got out of the cab and walked up to Valentine, who look more beautiful than the last time he saw her.

"Hey Mike," Valentine said.

"Hey, Valentine. And look at you." Knight knelt down to his daughter, who looked like Valentine.

Valentine had quit her job as an NYPD detective in the Bronx when she found out who Knight was and what she was up against. After moving to Chicago, she now worked for a big travel agency making good money.

Knight spent the whole day in Chuck-E-Cheese with his daughter and baby mother. Valentin didn't ask what he had going on because she had people in the NYPD headquarters and they told her everything.

Having Knight around touched her heart, but she knew better than to get used to it because he was still in the streets.

***

Atlanta, Georgia
Weeks later

Bree waited in a Caribbean food spot on the west side of Atlanta to meet someone.

Bree's people had retired from the game years ago but he told her this was the real deal and he put in a good word for her.

She saw a man walking to the place dressed like an African Muslim, but she paid him no mind.

When she saw the man sit down at a table next to her, she saw something unique about his style and swag.

Bree sat there for an hour, then got up and got ready to leave.

"Have a seat," the African man said, turning to face her now.

"Who the hell are you?" Bree asked with an attitude.

"I'm Khalid. You came to see me. I had to feel you out first. Please sit," Khalid said, ready to talk business. He had to make sure she was clean and wasn't working with the FBI or police.

Chapter 48
Flatbush, BK

Official's worker told him he got robbed by a nigga named Fats. Now he was on his way with two soldiers and a Yukon truck, ready to figure out why that nigga jacked him.

It was early in the morning and Official was ready to maim and murder. The beef with Fats and Money was quiet and he was waiting for the second they would pop up again.

Once on the block, Cory posted up on the steps nervously with a crazy look on his face.

"Yo, what happened, my G?" said Official, climbing out of the truck, telling his goons to stay inside.

"They took the coke and left the money and a note," Cory said, shaking with fear.

"Where is the note? And chill out, bro, it's cool. I'm going to take care of this, son. You good," Official said.

"The note inside," Cory said, walking into the building to an apartment on the first floor.

When Official opened the door and walked inside the dark apartment, he felt something was off. "Yo Cory, where's the note?" Official asked, seeing two niggas step out of the dark. It was 50 and Don with their guns drawn.

"Brooklyn's finest," Don said, pointing his gun at Official.

"This how you give it up, Cory?" Official asked. Cory couldn't even look him in his eyes.

"I'm sorry," were Cory's last words before 50 blew his brains out.

"I guess I'm next," Official repeated, seeing everybody drop.

"You guessed right," Fat said, coming out of the bathroom after taking a shit, not flushing the toilet.

Fats had showed Official the game. He got his first pack from Fats. He was like a father figure to him until shit went left.

"What a surprise," Official said with a frown.

"Y'all go outside. I got this, nephew," Fats told his crew.

"Nephew?" Official was confused.

"It's a long story. But don't hold your breath. You still look like money and smell like it too," Fats stated.

"If you want to talk, let's talk. If not, do me a solid and kill me, bitch!" Official was ready to die.

Boc! Boc! Boc! Boc! Boc!

"Faggot," Fats mumbled, walking out of the crib, glad to have his shit bag off.

***

Gun Hill projects, BX
Four months later

Less got out at a gas station to get some gas real quick before heading to the west side to meet Kazzy. Cassey was five months pregnant and she was driving him crazy, so he wanted to take him out to grab some drinks.

Business was good and everybody was eating and living life. The drama was still litty in the city, but niggas wasn't dying like that lately.

After he paid for the gas, he walked back outside to see a nigga cleaning his windshield. Niggas always did this to get money for food or drugs. Homeless people filled the streets all over New York City. There were so many bums that if a millionaire would give each of them a dollar they would go broke.

"I'm good. Kick rocks," Less said so the man would stop cleaning his window.

When Less locked eyes with the man who was cleaning his window, he reached for his weapon.

Uncle Pimp already had him surrounded by shooters, all females with assault rifles.

Tat! Tat! Tat! Tat! Tat!

The women and Uncle Pimp put over thirty holes in Less's body before leaving him splattered on the ground.

The police didn't come for close to thirty-five minutes to pick up the body of another dead black male.

***

Manhattan, NY
Two weeks later

Kazzy took Cassey to her doctor's appointment as he did twice a week in Manhattan. He had left his phone in the car and so he went out to get it, leaving Cassey in the waiting room. Cassey's nurse called her to the back so she could be seen by the doctors in a second.

Being pregnant was new to her. She was experiencing mixed emotions every minute, like in a movie. She sat down and no more than ten seconds later, a man came in the room with his back turned to her.

"Hey, Doctor," Cassey said before seeing Uncle Pimp turn around with a pistol in his hand with the silencer attached to it.

"You crossed me," Uncle Pimp said.

"I never crossed you if I was never with you."

Her words cut his heart.

Psst! Psst! Psst! Psst!

Uncle Pimp ran out of the room and creeped out the back exit. He had his people see that Cassey's Social Security number was being used at this clinic twice a month.

By the time Kazzy made it upstairs, people were trying to save Cassey and her seed, but she didn't make it.

Kazzy cried right there for an hour. He had plans to build a family with Cassey, but now she was gone.

Losing his seed hurt the worst because Kazzy was ready for that real balance in his life, but now it was gone.

***

Downtown, Brooklyn

Fats and his daughter sat in his condo eating dinner. He called D'Aray over to apologize for not telling her about Jadaya.

"I'm glad you came," he said.

"I guess." D'Aray had to sneak away from Jadaya and Paco to see what her dad wanted. D'Aray felt like she could at least hear him out. She had a good heart at times.

"I have a question, D'Aray."

"What is it?"

"You still fucking with Paco? You thought I wouldn't find out?" Fats didn't even give her a chance to reply before he shot her in the face seven times.

After he saw her body fall out of the chair, he continued to eat his shrimp. His walls were soundproof, so he wasn't worried about neighbors.

***

Brooklyn, NY

50 was in a strip club drunk, alone, thinking how far he came in life and how far he had to go to get where he wanted to be. He and Don were trying to find Knight and his crew, but Knight was too advanced.

50 admired how Knight moved. He was smart, but when he got ahold of him, he wasn't going to hesitate to knock his top off.

He got up, walking to the bathroom to see a bad bitch leaning on the wall and smiling at him.

"Are you trying to come in with me?" 50 said, almost falling over.

"You can't afford this," the woman said, looking him up and down.

"I got however much you want. I hope you can suck a good dick." He walked into the bathroom first and she walked in behind him, locking the door.

One thing 50 loved about New York was that the dancers would fuck you for the right price.

50 pulled out his dick and the woman pulled out a knife and attacked him, stabbing him in his heart, neck, and head.

By the time Red was done, blood was all over the floor as if a toilet had overrun or a pipe busted.

Red smoothly walked outside to where Lil K awaited her so they could go to the meeting. Knight awaited them.

Knight had some big news to tell them which could change the game.

To Be Continued…
Jack Boys Vs Dope Boys II
Coming Soon

Lock Down Publications and Ca$h Presents assisted pub-
lishing packages.

BASIC PACKAGE $499
Editing
Cover Design
Formatting

UPGRADED PACKAGE $800
Typing
Editing
Cover Design
Formatting

ADVANCE PACKAGE $1,200
Typing
Editing
Cover Design
Formatting
Copyright registration
Proofreading
Upload book to Amazon

LDP SUPREME PACKAGE $1,500
Typing
Editing
Cover Design
Formatting
Copyright registration
Proofreading
Set up Amazon account
Upload book to Amazon
Advertise on LDP Amazon and Facebook page

***Other services available upon request. Additional charges
may apply
Lock Down Publications
P.O. Box 944
Stockbridge, GA 30281-9998
Phone # 470 303-9761

Submission Guideline

Submit the first three chapters of your completed manuscript to ldpsub-missions@gmail.com, subject line: Your book's title. The manuscript must be in a .doc file and sent as an attachment. Document should be in Times New Roman, double spaced and in size 12 font. Also, provide your synopsis and full contact information. If sending multiple submissions, they must each be in a separate email.

Have a story but no way to send it electronically? You can still submit to LDP/Ca$h Presents. Send in the first three chapters, written or typed, of your completed manuscript to:

LDP: Submissions Dept
Po Box 944
Stockbridge, Ga 30281

DO NOT send original manuscript. Must be a duplicate.

Provide your synopsis and a cover letter containing your full contact information.

Thanks for considering LDP and Ca$h Presents.

NEW RELEASES

THE PLUG OF LIL MEXICO by CHRIS GREEN
THE STREETS STAINED MY SOUL 3 by MARCELLUS ALLEN
KING OF THE TRENCHES 2 by GHOST & TRANAY ADAMS
MOB TIES 5 by SAYNOMORE
KING KILLA by VINCENT "VITTO" HOLLOWAY
JACK BOYS VS DOPE BOYS by ROMELL TUKES

Romell Tukes

Coming Soon from Lock Down Publications/Ca$h Presents

BLOOD OF A BOSS **VI**

SHADOWS OF THE GAME II

TRAP BASTARD II

By **Askari**

LOYAL TO THE GAME **IV**

By **T.J. & Jelissa**

IF TRUE SAVAGE **VIII**

MIDNIGHT CARTEL IV

DOPE BOY MAGIC IV

CITY OF KINGZ III

NIGHTMARE ON SILENT AVE II

THE PLUG OF LIL MEXICO II

By **Chris Green**

BLAST FOR ME **III**

A SAVAGE DOPEBOY III

CUTTHROAT MAFIA III

DUFFLE BAG CARTEL VII

HEARTLESS GOON VI

By **Ghost**

A HUSTLER'S DECEIT III

KILL ZONE II

BAE BELONGS TO ME III

By **Aryanna**

KING OF THE TRAP III

By **T.J. Edwards**

GORILLAZ IN THE BAY V

3X KRAZY III

STRAIGHT BEAST MODE II

De'Kari

KINGPIN KILLAZ IV

STREET KINGS III

PAID IN BLOOD III

CARTEL KILLAZ IV

DOPE GODS III

Hood Rich

SINS OF A HUSTLA II

ASAD

RICH $AVAGE II

MONEY IN THE GRAVE II

By Martell Troublesome Bolden

YAYO V

Bred In The Game 2

S. Allen

CREAM III

By Yolanda Moore

SON OF A DOPE FIEND III

HEAVEN GOT A GHETTO II

By Renta

LOYALTY AIN'T PROMISED III

By Keith Williams

I'M NOTHING WITHOUT HIS LOVE II

SINS OF A THUG II

TO THE THUG I LOVED BEFORE II

By Monet Dragun

QUIET MONEY IV

EXTENDED CLIP III

THUG LIFE IV

By **Trai'Quan**

THE STREETS MADE ME IV

By **Larry D. Wright**

IF YOU CROSS ME ONCE II

By **Anthony Fields**

THE STREETS WILL NEVER CLOSE II

By **K'ajji**

HARD AND RUTHLESS III

THE BILLIONAIRE BENTLEYS II

Von Diesel

KILLA KOUNTY II

By **Khufu**

MONEY GAME III

By **Smoove Dolla**

JACK BOYS VS DOPE BOYS II

By **Romell Tukes**

MURDA WAS THE CASE II

Elijah R. Freeman

THE STREETS NEVER LET GO II

By **Robert Baptiste**

AN UNFORESEEN LOVE III

By **Meesha**

KING OF THE TRENCHES III
by **GHOST & TRANAY ADAMS**

MONEY MAFIA II

LOYAL TO THE SOIL II

By **Jibril Williams**

QUEEN OF THE ZOO II

By **Black Migo**

THE BRICK MAN IV

By **King Rio**

VICIOUS LOYALTY II

Jack Boys Vs. Dope Boys

By Kingpen

A GANGSTA'S PAIN II

By J-Blunt

CONFESSIONS OF A JACKBOY III

By Nicholas Lock

GRIMEY WAYS II

By Ray Vinci

KING KILLA II

By Vincent "Vitto" Holloway

Available Now

RESTRAINING ORDER **I & II**

By **CA$H & Coffee**

LOVE KNOWS NO BOUNDARIES **I II & III**

By **Coffee**

RAISED AS A GOON I, II, III & IV

BRED BY THE SLUMS I, II, III

BLAST FOR ME I & II

ROTTEN TO THE CORE I II III

A BRONX TALE I, II, III

DUFFLE BAG CARTEL I II III IV V VI

HEARTLESS GOON I II III IV V

A SAVAGE DOPEBOY I II

DRUG LORDS I II III

CUTTHROAT MAFIA I II

KING OF THE TRENCHES

By **Ghost**

LAY IT DOWN **I & II**

LAST OF A DYING BREED I II

BLOOD STAINS OF A SHOTTA I & II III

By **Jamaica**

LOYAL TO THE GAME I II III

LIFE OF SIN I, II III

By **TJ & Jelissa**

BLOODY COMMAS I & II

SKI MASK CARTEL I II & III

KING OF NEW YORK I II,III IV V

RISE TO POWER I II III

COKE KINGS I II III IV V

BORN HEARTLESS I II III IV

KING OF THE TRAP I II

By **T.J. Edwards**

IF LOVING HIM IS WRONG…I & II

LOVE ME EVEN WHEN IT HURTS I II III

By **Jelissa**

WHEN THE STREETS CLAP BACK I & II III

THE HEART OF A SAVAGE I II III

MONEY MAFIA

LOYAL TO THE SOIL

By **Jibril Williams**

A DISTINGUISHED THUG STOLE MY HEART I II & III

LOVE SHOULDN'T HURT I II III IV

RENEGADE BOYS I II III IV

Jack Boys Vs. Dope Boys

PAID IN KARMA I II III

SAVAGE STORMS I II

AN UNFORESEEN LOVE I II

By **Meesha**

A GANGSTER'S CODE I &, II III

A GANGSTER'S SYN I II III

THE SAVAGE LIFE I II III

CHAINED TO THE STREETS I II III

BLOOD ON THE MONEY I II III

A GANGSTA'S PAIN

By J-Blunt

PUSH IT TO THE LIMIT

By **Bre' Hayes**

BLOOD OF A BOSS **I, II, III, IV, V**

SHADOWS OF THE GAME

TRAP BASTARD

By **Askari**

THE STREETS BLEED MURDER **I, II & III**

THE HEART OF A GANGSTA I II& III

By **Jerry Jackson**

CUM FOR ME I II III IV V VI VII VIII

An **LDP Erotica Collaboration**

BRIDE OF A HUSTLA **I II & II**

THE FETTI GIRLS **I, II& III**

CORRUPTED BY A GANGSTA I, II III, IV

BLINDED BY HIS LOVE

THE PRICE YOU PAY FOR LOVE I, II ,III

DOPE GIRL MAGIC I II III

By **Destiny Skai**

WHEN A GOOD GIRL GOES BAD

Romell Tukes

By **Adrienne**
THE COST OF LOYALTY I II III
By Kweli
A GANGSTER'S REVENGE **I II III & IV**
THE BOSS MAN'S DAUGHTERS I II III IV V
A SAVAGE LOVE **I & II**
BAE BELONGS TO ME I II
A HUSTLER'S DECEIT I, II, III
WHAT BAD BITCHES DO I, II, III
SOUL OF A MONSTER I II III
KILL ZONE
A DOPE BOY'S QUEEN I II III
By **Aryanna**
A KINGPIN'S AMBITON
A KINGPIN'S AMBITION **II**
I MURDER FOR THE DOUGH
By **Ambitious**
TRUE SAVAGE I II III IV V VI VII
DOPE BOY MAGIC I, II, III
MIDNIGHT CARTEL I II III
CITY OF KINGZ I II
NIGHTMARE ON SILENT AVE
THE PLUG OF LIL MEXICO II

By **Chris Green**
A DOPEBOY'S PRAYER
By **Eddie "Wolf" Lee**
THE KING CARTEL **I, II & III**
By **Frank Gresham**
THESE NIGGAS AIN'T LOYAL **I, II & III**

200

Jack Boys Vs. Dope Boys

By **Nikki Tee**

GANGSTA SHYT **I II &III**

By **CATO**

THE ULTIMATE BETRAYAL

By **Phoenix**

BOSS'N UP **I , II & III**

By **Royal Nicole**

I LOVE YOU TO DEATH

By **Destiny J**

I RIDE FOR MY HITTA

I STILL RIDE FOR MY HITTA

By **Misty Holt**

LOVE & CHASIN' PAPER

By **Qay Crockett**

TO DIE IN VAIN

SINS OF A HUSTLA

By **ASAD**

BROOKLYN HUSTLAZ

By **Boogsy Morina**

BROOKLYN ON LOCK I & II

By **Sonovia**

GANGSTA CITY

By **Teddy Duke**

A DRUG KING AND HIS DIAMOND I & II III

A DOPEMAN'S RICHES

HER MAN, MINE'S TOO I, II

CASH MONEY HO'S

THE WIFEY I USED TO BE I II

By Nicole Goosby

TRAPHOUSE KING **I II & III**

KINGPIN KILLAZ I II III

STREET KINGS I II

PAID IN BLOOD **I II**

CARTEL KILLAZ I II III

DOPE GODS I II

By **Hood Rich**

LIPSTICK KILLAH **I, II, III**

CRIME OF PASSION I II & III

FRIEND OR FOE I II III

By **Mimi**

STEADY MOBBN' **I, II, III**

THE STREETS STAINED MY SOUL I II III

By **Marcellus Allen**

WHO SHOT YA **I, II, III**

SON OF A DOPE FIEND I II

HEAVEN GOT A GHETTO

Renta

GORILLAZ IN THE BAY **I II III IV**

TEARS OF A GANGSTA I II

3X KRAZY I II

STRAIGHT BEAST MODE

DE'KARI

TRIGGADALE I II III

MURDAROBER WAS THE CASE

Elijah R. Freeman

GOD BLESS THE TRAPPERS I, II, III

THESE SCANDALOUS STREETS I, II, III

FEAR MY GANGSTA I, II, III IV, V

THESE STREETS DON'T LOVE NOBODY I, II

BURY ME A G I, II, III, IV, V

Jack Boys Vs. Dope Boys

A GANGSTA'S EMPIRE I, II, III, IV

THE DOPEMAN'S BODYGAURD I II

THE REALEST KILLAZ I II III

THE LAST OF THE OGS I II III

Tranay Adams

THE STREETS ARE CALLING

Duquie Wilson

MARRIED TO A BOSS I II III

By Destiny Skai & Chris Green

KINGZ OF THE GAME I II III IV V VI

Playa Ray

SLAUGHTER GANG I II III

RUTHLESS HEART I II III

By Willie Slaughter

FUK SHYT

By Blakk Diamond

DON'T F#CK WITH MY HEART I II

By Linnea

ADDICTED TO THE DRAMA I II III

IN THE ARM OF HIS BOSS II

By Jamila

YAYO I II III IV

A SHOOTER'S AMBITION I II

BRED IN THE GAME

By S. Allen

TRAP GOD I II III

RICH $AVAGE

MONEY IN THE GRAVE I II

By Martell Troublesome Bolden

FOREVER GANGSTA

Romell Tukes

GLOCKS ON SATIN SHEETS I II
By Adrian Dulan
TOE TAGZ I II III
LEVELS TO THIS SHYT I II
By Ah'Million
KINGPIN DREAMS I II III
By Paper Boi Rari
CONFESSIONS OF A GANGSTA I II III IV
CONFESSIONS OF A JACKBOY I II
By Nicholas Lock
I'M NOTHING WITHOUT HIS LOVE
SINS OF A THUG
TO THE THUG I LOVED BEFORE
A GANGSTA SAVED XMAS
By Monet Dragun
CAUGHT UP IN THE LIFE I II III
THE STREETS NEVER LET GO
By Robert Baptiste
NEW TO THE GAME I II III
MONEY, MURDER & MEMORIES I II III
By **Malik D. Rice**
LIFE OF A SAVAGE I II III
A GANGSTA'S QUR'AN I II III
MURDA SEASON I II III
GANGLAND CARTEL I II III
CHI'RAQ GANGSTAS I II III
KILLERS ON ELM STREET I II III
JACK BOYZ N DA BRONX I II III
A DOPEBOY'S DREAM I II III
JACK BOYS VS DOPE BOYS

Jack Boys Vs. Dope Boys

By **Romell Tukes**

LOYALTY AIN'T PROMISED I II

By Keith Williams

QUIET MONEY I II III

THUG LIFE I II III

EXTENDED CLIP I II

By **Trai'Quan**

THE STREETS MADE ME I II III

By **Larry D. Wright**

THE ULTIMATE SACRIFICE I, II, III, IV, V, VI

KHADIFI

IF YOU CROSS ME ONCE

ANGEL I II

IN THE BLINK OF AN EYE

By **Anthony Fields**

THE LIFE OF A HOOD STAR

By Ca$h & Rashia Wilson

THE STREETS WILL NEVER CLOSE

By K'ajji

CREAM I II

By Yolanda Moore

NIGHTMARES OF A HUSTLA I II III

By King Dream

CONCRETE KILLA I II

VICIOUS LOYALTY

By Kingpen

HARD AND RUTHLESS I II

MOB TOWN 251

THE BILLIONAIRE BENTLEYS

By Von Diesel

GHOST MOB

Stilloan Robinson

MOB TIES I II III IV V

By SayNoMore

BODYMORE MURDERLAND I II III

By Delmont Player

FOR THE LOVE OF A BOSS

By C. D. Blue

MOBBED UP I II III IV

THE BRICK MAN I II III

By King Rio

KILLA KOUNTY

By Khufu

MONEY GAME I II

By Smoove Dolla

A GANGSTA'S KARMA I II

By FLAME

KING OF THE TRENCHES I II

by **GHOST & TRANAY ADAMS**

QUEEN OF THE ZOO

By **Black Migo**

GRIMEY WAYS

By Ray Vinci

XMAS WITH AN ATL SHOOTER

By Ca$h & Destiny Skai

KING KILLA

By Vincent "Vitto" Holloway

BOOKS BY LDP'S CEO, CA$H

TRUST IN NO MAN

TRUST IN NO MAN 2

TRUST IN NO MAN 3

BONDED BY BLOOD

SHORTY GOT A THUG

THUGS CRY

THUGS CRY 2

THUGS CRY 3

TRUST NO BITCH

TRUST NO BITCH 2

TRUST NO BITCH 3

TIL MY CASKET DROPS

RESTRAINING ORDER

RESTRAINING ORDER 2

IN LOVE WITH A CONVICT

LIFE OF A HOOD STAR

XMAS WITH AN ATL SHOOTER

Romell Tukes